MY BROTHER ⬚ N

D. JAMES SMITH

[signature: D. James Smith]

THE PERMANENT PRESS
SAG HARBOR, NEW YORK, 11963

Copyright© 2004 by D. James Smith

Library of Congress Cataloging-in-Publication Data

Smith, D.J., 1955-
    My brothers passion : a novel / by D. James Smith.
      p. cm.
    ISBN 1-57962-107-4 (alk. paper)
    1. Boys—Fiction. 2. Brothers—Fiction. 3. Violence—Fiction.
    4. Korean Americans—Fiction. 5. Children of clergy—
    Fiction. 6. Vietnamese Conflict, 1961-1975—Veterans—
    Fiction. I. Title.

    PS3659.M51697M9 2004
    813'.54—dc22

                            2003066878

Printed in The United States of America

THE PERMANENT PRESS
4170 Noyac Road
Sag Harbor, NY 11963

I would like to acknowledge The National Endowment for the Arts for a fellowship which aided in the completion of this book, and, too, for their welcomed help: Annette Fiel, Richard W. Jackson, Sonya Janian, Rod Paul, Josephine Redlin, Teresina Smith, and Liza Wieland.

Also, I must thank Judith and Martin Shepard for making it possible in such genteel fashion,

Barbara Markowitz, my agent, for her counsel and encouragement,

Linda St. John for her generosity and art,

and, of course, Kimberly, who always believed.

..............................for Glen

MY BROTHER'S PASSION

For The Arnie Nixon
Center.

All best,
David

The first time I saw my brother's passion was when we drove Glen downtown to the train station. Of course I didn't know who she was then. We were all in our bus, the '67 Volkswagen, the only new thing my dad ever bought. Mother was up front, sniffling to herself in the passenger seat, and my dad had his eyes trapped in the rearview mirror, trying to memorize Glen's face. He never wanted my brother to go, always said something about this thing not being a game, not dominoes, not a theory at all.

We were crossing town quickly that day, turning west at the cathedral where the idolaters gathered every Sunday to look at their statues and get their orders from the pope. On account of my dad, we were Baptists and knew that sweet Jesus had no bargain with priests, that you could give up your own heart yourself to His mercy and get some relief. Even though my brother got saved the week before he shipped out, went down in the mystery and came up sputtering in the glass pool that was built alongside one wall of First Baptist, stood there blinking out at my folks and all the rest of us in our pews, I could see in his eyes that it hadn't taken, that he'd come up afraid.

We went on west of downtown where things scattered out, shops and industrial buildings and the gray grain silos towering along the tracks. We drove all the way without talking, Glen giving me a wink once in awhile. With his Levis, and his Beatle haircut just beginning to grow long, he looked good, though I wasn't paying the sort of attention I should've on a day like that; mostly I was fiddling with my transistor radio plugged in one ear listening to kids calling in, wanting to hear their sweetheart's name on the air.

The Stones were getting no satisfaction whatsoever, and Jim Morrison was wishing his baby would light him up over and over, which made me think of the monk, some kind of priest, who'd poured gasoline all over himself right there on CBS. That happened back when I was still a little kid. He did it to himself on a street corner over there, making his whole life into a fire of love for his people. We were all eating in the living room and my dad's entire head turned pink like salmon when that came on. Made him slam down his fork and just clean leave the room.

Mother was pained, you could tell, because her voice was like glass breaking when she told me to turn off the Magnavox. She didn't eat any more, just watched Glen, who was maybe fifteen or sixteen back then but already itching to go. He finished off his meat loaf without flinching, trying to show he wasn't surprised by all that was going on over there.

The monk was all love, my mother explained that night when I couldn't sleep. Sometimes, love is tricky. She said it wasn't for free. Said it could ask more from you than you thought when you started out with your love. One thing could fall into another and things could go awful and wrong, I guess, which is the domino theory all over again.

My father would say all this is an old story and not worth the trouble.Say it's all in the Old Testament should I bother to look. But I say, it never happened to me till it did, and, sometimes, it's still fresh to the point of hurting, the way things that you need usually are. And there's some that don't know and they should as there's solace in that. The Bible's still going on every day if you look.

I don't know what my brother would say if he were still talking. He's just like those bits of light drilling holes through the roof of our garage and that roof like the top of my head, that light going all the way to my heart and the reason for all that I'm telling.

When we got to the train station, that woman was there, out front, red hair rolled up on her head, holding a cigarette in one hand, fingernails painted the color of cranberries. She was smiling like a sunbeam— even the air around her looking warm—and she was talking to some guy in a rumpled green suit when she glanced at us pulling up to the curb. Her face froze for a second, and, quick as quick, she flicked her blue eyes from my brother to my mom in the front seat. Then she turned and took the green suit by the arm and walked away slowly, and I turned to my brother, trying to see what was what but his face wasn't telling.

That was Glen's way, the way of my mother and her people. They're there every day on the mantle at home in their little rosewood frames, and their faces are smoothed out and their eyes wouldn't tell you nothing even if you could put torture on them directly. They never show their desire. That's Asian. That's smart. That is, if you want to get by in this world. It's just ignorance if you think otherwise. I know that much.

I know for certain that I wish that when things change, they wouldn't change for good. I wish we'd never moved away the way we did in the end. I wish we hadn't had to. I wish I'd never seen all that struggle and killing. I could have never planned on Erin Bleecher being dead or that Jew or on what happened to Uncle Aquilla. And I wish I'd never found my brother the way I finally did. I never set out to understand about desire and the things it'll make you do when it gets out of hand, starts its burning you up, the way it did all of them.

*   *   *   *

It was October when my brother went off, October when that rain started. Started slow and gentle, sifting down soft as grace, a fine swept rain, clicking on top of the aluminum roof of the carport, the kind of rain that you have to look hard at to actually see. Look hard into the distance, 'cause you can hear it sort of mouthing the puddles and you can feel it settling on your face, but you can't really see it, unless you angle your eyes so that the little splinters of light catch it and bring it out against the dark needles of a pine, or the flat leaves of the magnolias, or the drooping branches of the eucalyptus, the trees planted up back of our place.

Of course, that was just the start of it. Within a couple of weeks, it was hurtling down *without pity*, my mother said. Down every day and most nights too, for most of that month. Down in a way everybody said was unusual, down in a way it did only one other time, much later—though I didn't know that then, that it would rain both times—when my brother went away for good in the end. It came down sogging the ground so that when you walked around, the earth would suck at you, make a sucking sound when you lifted your boots. It's not supposed to rain much in California, not in the valley because at one time this place was a desert, that is, before it became *God's own miracle,* my father would say—irrigation, modern methods of farming. But it did it anyway, in spite of its record, in spite of itself, came down and swelled all the ditches that ran through town, rose in the gutters and crept up on the lawns and lapped at the edges of everyone's houses.

It made my folks kind of twitchy, cooped up in the house, my mother burning incense for the ancestors, my dad grinding his pipe with his big corn-colored teeth, going out on the front porch to stare at the sky, not wanting to come in, worrying himself more than he should. Not that we farmed—we didn't have any crop to lose, but it was bad for the town, bad for the P. F. Stanley & Co. Bad for Uncle Aquilla who ran P.F. Stanley, and bad for the men who depended on the tractors and pickers they built.

My father said maybe our troubles were Biblical, but said we'd haul through, said most things work out if you leave them alone, leave them to God, though I wondered why those two things would be the same. Mostly, I remember the tiny sparrows that crowded the big monkeypuzzle just outside of our house who seemed stunned and interrupted and unhappy about the rain. Packed in there close as leaves, they were a whole slickered city of chattering and flicking and unease. And I watched them from my window and hoped for them the best.

*   *   *   *

I wouldn't shoot a sparrow, though I kept my eyes out for all sorts of birds. Long before that rain ever came, I was used to seeing them, mostly big fat pigeons with shining green throats, strutting around in the gutters that ended on our block because ours was the last block before you were in true country— miles and miles of flat open farmland and telephone poles tacked along the roads like toothpicks going out forever. Doves were pretty and their wings made a whistling when they rose off the ground, but they were stupid and easy to shoot, which I did all the time. My rifle was a good one, expensive, with a real wooden stock that shot steel pellets, a real prize as I was still only eleven going on twelve when I got it. My brother gave it to me just before he joined up and went overseas.

There were robins with soft apricot breasts and bluebirds that flickered like blue flames in the bushes. And there were crows. Before my brother went off, it was so dry deer came down from the hills looking for water and something to eat, and he shot one in a cornfield early one morning and strung it up from its hind legs in a eucalyptus that was back of our place. When I got up and came out of the house, I saw it there with its pretty little feet hanging down fine and dainty. My mother walked out there with me and my brother and there were a couple of crows stepping around on its rump being spiteful and noisy. And me and Glen chucked rocks at them till they lifted, pissed-off and rowing away ever so slowly with their pointy black-fingered wings. My mom said softly to Glen, "Honey, hurry up and get that poor thing dressed out and away from my yard." And my brother nodded to her in his usual way, quiet and willing.

My brother's face was just like my mother's,

skin the color of peeled almonds and high rounded cheeks, eyes that were narrow and Asian. *White niggers* I'd heard people whisper downtown, some farmer or salesman or mother with pasty-faced, runny-nosed kids, whisper it just loud enough to be heard, then turn away to study a cantaloupe or onion at the grocery. I looked like my dad, round eyes, blue eyes, thin white skin that flushed red as a brick when we were mad or embarrassed.

My dad said just ignore it when I heard that. He said that was ignorance, that our whole town was mixed—Okies, Italians, Armenians, Mexicans, even Japanese, so being Korean wasn't really anything different round here. But it troubled me some. My mom was so pretty you'd think they could see it. She was a gentle one, small and usually dressed really smart even when she was around the house in the evenings when she wore her hair down, gleaming black hair, long and showy, silk pajamas, a black robe with a green dragon growing up from her feet.

And the town did look like it had been built by a jumble of people. It spread out without any plan, just one street downtown and some churches and neighborhoods arranged around it with the railroad splitting the whole thing, crooked. Trains stopped traffic most anytime they wanted to when they rumbled through, rusted and loud. At night, you could hear their horns-long, heart-tight, sorrowful sounds. Dad said say what you will but it was better than living in the dirt which he understood on account he was born up in the hills of Tennessee. Glen would say our grandmother on that side, who I'd never seen,

16

used to smoke her own pipe made out of clay, but that could've been a lie as he was forever fond of pulling my leg. I suppose I should have resented it, but when he got to telling me a story, letting it circle around on the ceiling before he dropped it down over me like a trick lasso, his eyes would get wet in the corners with laughter, and even when I knew it was my leg getting yanked, I'd let him go on thinking I was younger and dumber than I was just so as to see him happy like that.

Our house had town on one side and country on the other. An orchard of almonds took off from the thick wild grass of our place, and after the almonds a wide ditch for irrigation snaked through a field of grapes and after that there were onions and so on and on.

Uncle Aquilla lived up the street on the other side of us in a big brick house with white shutters. The house had a drive that was blacktopped smooth, and it was edged, too, with brick, and everyone said it looked fine—had a front porch with white columns and one of the few lawns in our whole town that wasn't Bermuda. Aquilla had long, fine, shiny grass he was proud of. Himself, he was nearly six feet four, a lot bigger than my father. He was shop foreman at the plant and got my dad his job. He was the kind of guy who stopped people talking whenever he came around. Men would sort of shuffle and nod and wait on him to speak which he didn't do very much. They'd scratch their necks, real thoughtful, and after he'd leave the air would clear up and their faces would soften and somebody or other would crack wise and their laughter would come, quick and relieved.

I knew Uncle Aquilla didn't think much of my mother 'cause he never came to dinner and we didn't go over there much, and if we did it was just my dad and me. Even Glen seemed to gall him. Seemed just the sight of him made Aquilla polite as a stranger, mouth puckered up and sour, little pockets of discouragement under his cheeks. I think that sort of thing made my mom fond of Glen especially, kind of weak with him and careful.

That's why she was gentle as ever with him that morning, about getting rid of that deer, saying, *Honey* to him, though it was a horror to her, hanging there in her yard. I got to help with that deer. Glen split its belly with his buck knife and the insides slumped out, warm and smoking. "Dave, get me that short-handled ax, will you?" he said so I ran for the shed out back of our garage. I remember that after we'd stripped back the skin, he used the ax to separate the muscles near the bones where the legs joined the body, the ax making a dull *chump, chumping* sound in the cold. When we first started, I thought that deer was watching us, one big mirror-black eye rolled back like it was curious until I looked closer and saw that there wasn't anything there, just a clear patch of sky, open and running free in all that dark space.

It wasn't that long before we got letters. They came ever so often. I remember one from South Carolina and then maybe some months later, one from Maryland, Virginia. But I know it was a good long time before we got one from clear overseas, even later when we got an actual phone call coming all those thousands of miles through a cable my dad said was laid out like plumbing on the floor of the ocean. Glen said the heat there was bad as it was at home in the summers except that it wasn't dry, said the air could cling to your skin like cellophane wrapping, said, *That's the Nam for you.* He said not ever to worry, wrote it in a letter, *Dave, don't you worry, I got plenty of buddies here. Say, I bet you'd go crazy about the birds over here, you can't imagine the colors.* Though soon enough I could imagine them, or leastways I tried, because I went to the city library and found a book about the birds they have over there. I got a notebook with thick paper at the five and dime and started in on drawing them, too.

Sometimes I'd dream them all flying around our house, coming to sit in the trees like a hundred colored rags, unfurled and flapping in the breeze. And I'd run around the place thinking, if Glen's birds were there, then he must be round there somewhere himself, and then I figured out that wasn't possible so I made up a lie for myself, made it up right in the middle of one of those dreams and kept it the next morning and from then on. And it was this: when the birds showed up that was a sign that, just then, at that very moment, he was over there and thinking about us, imagining us same as I would when I'd picture him.

That's the kind of lie you can tell to yourself because it's possibly good as the truth. Otherwise, where would a lie like that come from? You shouldn't forsake something that comes in your head of its own, comes with that power.

That rain we'd had wasn't normal. It's dry most of the time around there. Dry enough that all that water was drunk up pretty soon by the soil In fact, in winter, before the snow in the mountains melted off, the canals in the valley always went dry. I liked to walk down the road till I came to a ditch and then climb down inside and follow it for as long as I could, out to hell and gone, until I got tired or it got dark and I'd have to head home. I got to carrying a flashlight 'cause I'd get so distracted I might not start back until it was pitch black. There was all manner of stuff down there—old mattresses, tires, half rusted-away barrels, dead cats and skunks, even a Ford Model A with all the chrome pitted green and black like abalone and just springs for a seat. It was a bombed-out highway I had to myself. They say never walk the canals because you can't know when the guys running the dam might bleed off water from the lake and you could get drowned, though I never saw that.

I liked to walk off as far as I could and then climb out somewhere I'd never seen, come up in somebody's field and sneak up on their place and see how they lived. It was a habit I got into, and I can say it put some shame on me, but I couldn't stop it and figured no one really cared. I'd come up close on a house, crawling on my belly through grass or whatever they were growing, and I'd watch while the sun shriveled up like an old tangerine in the haze on the edge of the world. And the shadows would start stretching, and then they'd step slowly out from the trees, and the lights in the houses would come on, and I could get close enough to peek inside. My heart would start thumping for no reason I know, 'cause the folks in those places weren't doing much but the usual stuff. But I felt some kind of thrill like I was watching my own little play, the folks moving around in the windows like puppets, and I'd think to myself, I am watching, like God.

*   *   *   *

Glen did what everyone wanted. That was his way. I see there's those that have to do what others won't let themselves. The least of things. The hardest. That's fate. I'd say those that have it, have a loneliness more than most. But Glen didn't have to do all that he did. What was forbidden and wrong. But, I didn't know that yet.

I was just waiting for him, spending lots of that time putting a watch and a study on things. Probably that time went by slowly, but I don't remember most of it, so in my head it was quick. I was growing, which happens without your having to notice it. But I did do some study on things and those I have with me fresh. Some of that study was curiosity, some mischief, and some of it just vanity. In the mirror, I'd see I really was like my father— curly blond hair, clear blue eyes like marbles, a nose that was knobbed round on its end and dotted with blackheads like a strawberry.

I had a room upstairs, to myself, with a ceiling that slanted down toward my bed. It was all tongue and groove cedar, the walls and the ceiling. The window was next to the bed and gave me a view of the yard. There was a bathroom next to my room and my brother's room next to that and that's all. I was supposed to go up or down stairs and stay put, not run up and down and make a lot of racket so sometimes I got stuck up there longer than I liked.

On one wall I had a picture of a pheasant scared out of a yellow field. Mother said that picture was special. The Book of Changes, *a holy book,* she said, told how a flying pheasant was a symbol of forms changing, though looking at it, then, I could still think of the .410 shotgun I wanted and would have needed to bring down something big as it was. On the other wall, my dad hung a picture of Jesus—blond, blue-eyed, face of a girl. Next to that I had a picture I'd made as a kid and still liked: layers of crayolas scratched down with a pin—a boy standing in front of a house, a sunflower growing next to him, a burning yellow wheel in a sky I'd streaked red and blue.

Downstairs we had a big kitchen with enough room to feed a crew of workers, and I suppose in that house at one time that's just what they'd done.There was a living room with leaded glass doors that rolled out of the walls and closed off the rest of the house if my father wanted quiet. There was a parlor my mother had painted red where she kept the ancestors above a small fireplace we never lit. There were varnished tablets sitting on wooden stands where the names were carved. There were photographs, too; she kept water and rice in little green bowls that were set in black lacquer pedestals in front of the old faces.

I know my father didn't care for any of that, but you could tell he couldn't bear to see my mother unhappy, so he left it alone. With Glen gone the place seemed especially empty in a way I can't explain, maybe like the hole that's left in the air when somebody's passed by.

Mostly, I liked the basement. It was damp, smelled of wood beams and dust, and was ringed with shelves of old glass gallon wine jugs, the wine drunk up, the jugs refilled with water so in case the Russians went mad and sent us the bomb we'd have scads of fresh water. My dad had also a little shop for himself down there, a workbench and some tools. There was a little drawer there with a false bottom lined with red felt that had a Smith and Wesson .38 in it because my dad had once been a deputized sheriff for the county which he said didn't mean much except a few extra bucks when he used to walk the high school's parking lot at the football games on Friday nights in the fall.

I liked that you could crawl under the house from the basement and listen to the footsteps and muffled voices coming through the floor. I saw how the space between things was pretty thin, how things were connected and how things could slip back and forth like those voices and footsteps. And it made some sense to me that my mother left stuff out for her family, in spite of the truth of them being dead.

One night when I was down there in the basement doing I don't know what the phone rang. My dad had an extension down there because when he was working on something he couldn't be bothered climbing the stairs. So I waited a little and then picked up.

"God damn it, you keep that Jew away from the shop," Aquilla was saying.

"He'll get to them one way or another. That's his job for Christ sakes. He's supposed to organize. And just so you know, the men are listening to him. They've got reason to." Then a long pause. "He comes in Jack's Place you know, buys rounds sometimes." My father's voice was brittle, but quiet on the line.

"Just be damn sure you keep *your* nose clean. Keep clear of this thing.There can't be any family involved in this. That's all that I'm saying."

"I know what you're saying," my dad snapped back.

"Now don't get mad," my uncle said, irritated, talking down to my dad.

"I can't afford to get mad," my father said.

"Well, don't forget it."

Silence. I wondered if they were listening to see if I was on there, too. But I guess not because finally my uncle says, "How's everything else? Hear anything from your boy?"

"He's OK." I could feel my father freezing up.

"Still don't see why he'd want to go over there and mix things up with his own people."

"Just stop it right there, you hear me, Quill?" My dad's voice was shaky with fury.

"Now hold on, I didn't mean anything by that." I couldn't tell if he was purposeful—baiting my father—or if that was more of his own ignorant self.

Dad answered him back, sharp. "Just don't forget I'm in the middle of this. I'm on the line with these guys every day, not you." Then he just hung up.

That was the first time I heard about the Jew, way before I saw him around and long before I saw him with my own eyes, lying in the ditch with his hands tied behind him with baling wire, his feet cut off, and his head face-down in a puddle of dirty water, my brother's passion kneeling next to him crying, awful as an animal would, long before I'd grown up, before I'd seen real evil, with my own eyes, the Biblical kind.

*   *   *   *

So I thought that was that. Dad didn't ever talk about work, and I was back missing Glen hard, those months of that winter going by with me noticing and not noticing, the watching of that time kind of like watching sky. You watch sky and you won't see it moving unless you pick something to measure it by. Pick a cloud, nail it with your eye and you'll see it's moving, coming past the chimney or something, inching along toward who knows where. You have to notice 'cause what's going on seems slow, but it's not. Look away and look back and the whole sky could've changed, the whole world.

So it was some Saturday that I thought was going to be slow as sky when right after breakfast my dad said, "Get in the van." We were all in the kitchen and my mom was standing at the window washing dishes and didn't bat an eye or even look around, so I knew it was something they'd decided on already between themselves. And that's when I found out what I did about P.F. Stanley & Co.

Nobody worked Saturdays, so when we pulled up there weren't any cars in that big gravel parking lot, our tires making a chewing sound as we rolled up on the place. It was a monster, a cathedral of tin stretching out for at least two blocks with some flat-roofed buildings spoked out behind it. Dad had keys with him that opened a door down in the side of it, a little door opening into the belly where we stepped in where it was all dark and hushed with metal gleaming and the smell of oil and cold concrete underfoot.

I followed my dad down the long aisles, looking at the big machinery, complicated and twisted as the insides of a gigantic clock. It was cold in there, but I had my bombardier jacket on, one of those with the fake fur for a collar and some insignias patched on the arms. We went down the line, all the way, me following dad, without talking, my head swiveling round trying to take it all in.

Dad stopped sudden and pushed his cap back on his head and looked into a space between these big rollers. He squatted down and motioned me to him and he put his hand on my arm at the elbow and he pointed in there and I looked. "Your cousin, Marty, got caught in there back in fifty-two. Chewed him up. It was like cleaning up spaghetti. You see?" he said.

And I nodded, though I can't say I did. "Line was shut down for no more than four hours. Can you believe that, four hours?" I thought about that and maybe I got it, because my dad was watching my face and after a minute he seemed satisfied and patted my shoulder and stood up. He looked down at me, his blue eyes giving me a bright flash and me opening mine wide to take it. "I'm not ashamed of my life, but you got to know right now, you won't work here. Nope. Never."

OK, I nodded, sure, I understand, though the truth is I didn't see any shame in that place. We walked on down to the end of the building and through a door and into a place where the ceiling wasn't nearly as high and there was some finished-up stuff, lined up for shipping. I think they were pickers of some kind. They looked like giant grasshoppers crouched on their hind legs, folded up, big elbows of painted steel, jaws out front just itching to chew cotton. He said to go on and climb around on the stuff if I wanted, long as I didn't fall and get myself killed. Said he'd be back directly and walked back through the door we'd come in.

I scrambled up on one of those things, the whole situation science fiction, like one of them might start up of itself and run amok and turn me into spaghetti like cousin Marty. I got up top of it and into a little glass cabin there for the driver and closed the door and smelled the upholstery and pulled on the wheel, making believe I was driving. Soon enough, I noticed from up there I had a view through a window that was set in above the doorway that gave me a square shot of the line. Into that square steps my dad with a pry bar, or something that looks like one, and he's shoving it deep into the heart of the line, ramming it in solid, and I can tell that if they were to start up the works it would be trouble. It was plain that bar would go round, getting scrunched and things might back up and crunch down one upon another, and then it was I saw that my dad was giving P.F. Stanley & Co. some of the domino theory, all by himself.

*   *   *   *

I didn't plan on climbing out of the ditch one evening and finding the little wooden house where my brother's passion lived by herself. I wish I could have stopped myself from watching her after that first time, most any day that I could, going by to check on her, seeing her walking by the yellow windows, her red hair hovering round her head and

29

shoulders and her lavender slips and breasts upturned and perfectly fine like the best of fresh peaches. I understand why those men came around. I could tell she had some special pull, something invisible but real like the moon is supposed to have, tugging all the water that's here on this earth. I saw it said MaryAnn Sheeney on the mailbox. Painted on that tin cylinder at the end of her drive, painted careful, in red nail polish and even that gave me a little thump in my chest, wanting to know her as I did.

Sometimes those evenings the sky would grow, these canyons of purple and black swelling up, the first stars blinking alive overhead, sun leaking off into nothing, and I would lie in the grass thinking, listening to the wind picking up the leaves and rustling them around in the dark, me thinking about how hard it must be on the Lord to keep track of the wheat and the chaff, how hard it must be to separate all the things in this world that seemed to me all hung tight together. I know that was my mother's mind. She'd say, *It takes heads and tails to make one coin. It's notions of your own that says one side is good and the other bad.* Of course that would just make my dad mad and the back of his throat uncomfortable because he'd go to clearing it with a little hack. Or else she'd say, *Desire, there's the trouble.* Liked to say that. Made her feel she was her own self and had some thoughts. It was a subject my dad wouldn't touch out of respect. She knew that.

Lying there in the grass, the world going dark, I wondered why the Jew was trouble, why it was that he was around MaryAnn Sheeney more than anyone. Wondered what she saw in him. I tried to figure out what it was about him that made him what he was, how you could tell. The best I could make out was that his shirts were always white, with the collars buttoned down and his pants creased sharp like the men downtown. He had these beautiful shoes, the kind they call wingtips, buffed-up prideful, gloss-black and smooth:

Those wingtips must be expensive because there weren't many around that had them. Other than that, it's a fact I can say, he didn't look anything special. Not special as she was.

She had something that put me in mind of the Rose of Sharon my mother had, trussed up at home on some sticks. I don't know if it was a real Rose of Sharon, but she always said it was, and she admired it especially. I understand a fondness like that. There's flowers like that that'll open out, like it was just for you, and that's a loveliness that won't be ignored. Some guys say that's how it is the first time you lie down with a woman. You think it's just for you and it never happened that way for anybody, but as it's only your first, it's illusion.

If that's what happened to Glen with his passion, if she was for him the first time he saw loveliness, really saw it—like seeing those special, difficult colors of flowers, that softness spreading open like a bit of God's glory put in this world, your mind could seize on that little bit, even if God was just flicking it off, the way a bird flicks pieces of water off its wings and doesn't even know it's doing it—that's not illusion, especially if you had all that ugliness

31

Glen did, coming right after, over there, clear down the bottom of Asia.

*   *   *   *

Walking home from school on a day I stayed late for my choir practice, I crossed Jensen Ave., two blocks up from P. F. Stanley & Co. I went slow trying to see what I could, though I was careful about getting close because my folks had forbid it. I could tell there was a crowd, and the men out front were bumping shoulders like penned cattle, though not much sound came up the block. So I went down that way, even though I wasn't supposed to, sliding along the sidewalk along the fronts of the stores, my shadow following like a twin in the glass windows.

I was maybe a half block from them, and I could see the Jew was shouting into a bullhorn like the kind the lifeguards used at the municipal swimming pool in summer. His dark hair was curling off the top of his head like a flaming black candle. He was pointing with one finger into the air. I was watching so close and not paying attention to where I was going that I bumped into the old guys out front of

Nelson's Hardware & Tire, the ones who always wore flannel shirts and baseball caps and Redwing boots that didn't show any wear, which I suppose was on account of they didn't have to work anymore. They were out front of the tire shop getting what sun that they could. *Sit down, boy*, they said and I did, liking how their bench was a front row seat, that I wouldn't be noticed sitting there with them. We sat there, those guys spitting chew toward the gutter, spitting it out in a way that looked offhand but took practice and which I admired.

Across and down the way, the P. F. Stanley & Co. men were keen on what the Jew was saying, heads up toward him because he'd climbed onto the bed of a pickup doing, I guess, what organizers do. Ever once in awhile a cheer would go up, and the Jew would smile and shake his head with satisfaction, full of the devil, a little pinched laugh in his face that was half fun and half anger. I kept an eye for my dad, but didn't see him anywhere though he might've been there as that was a crowd. Three squad cars were parked, butted up together across the street from the men, but they stayed put, those policemen not even getting out.

It didn't seem that there was all that much happening, mostly watching—the men watching the Jew and the cops watching the crowd and the old guys watching the whole of it, and of course me watching too, and the Jew was taking note of everybody and everything, out of the corner of his eye, looking out for one and all. I wasn't that surprised to see Uncle Aquilla too, sitting in his old, polished

DeSoto, the one my aunt usually drove, in an alley-
way next to Alfred's Vacuum Repair, his jaw punched
out and his eyes squinted as if counting up the
thoughts in his head, separating them out and weigh-
ing them, you could tell, calm, like my mother would
say, calm as a man drained of mercy.

*   *   *   *

Mr. Cobley liked for us to sing full out for all we
were worth. Sing out making our lips round and perfect so the music would be perfect. He said he
expected our best, wanted us to feel the glory in
things the way he did. He threw his arms around a
lot, shoulders hunched forward, his face soulful, the
young Mr. Percy going along with us on the piano.
There were some who said that a long time ago Mr.
Cobley conducted up in the city of San Francisco,
until they wouldn't have him anymore because of
his drinking which was plain enough to see still had
him bound up in its sin. His face was chock full of
little veins that ran just beneath the surface of his
skin that was as thin as the rice paper my mother
used when she wrote overseas to her sister and then

34

later to Glen. You could smell the gin coming off of his arms, leaking out of the pores, his hands soft as oil and trembling when he talked.

But sometimes he'd join in and sing with us, his eyes lighting up with the beauty and his voice wouldn't quaver and there was a kind of holiness filling him up so it seemed that power was too much for him, him being shaky with his weakness for pleasure, and I thought the Baptists might be right 'cause I saw how things could fight themselves out, the power and the glory, the good and the bad, right there in front of you, if you just opened your eyes and took a good look.

*   *   *   *

Just walked out is what my dad said, puffed up brash, sudden, in a way that wasn't his way, not the usual for him, said it to my mother, her looking hurt and worried that day and from then on. I remember that right. *A definite strike,* he repeated, looking at her as if he wanted her to see he still had some fire, wasn't as old as she thought.

That got him started with his waiting out the

powers of P. F. Stanley & Co., and my mom got a job at a packing house. She glued labels to wooden boxes made for peaches. They'd need those boxes, plenty of them come summer, and so liked to get started early. She worked twelve hours a day, seven days a week for awhile, and then she'd be home for two days solid, mostly sleeping. Dad and I would keep ourselves quiet, not even running the washer or dryer, no color TV, not even talking. He was keen on teaching me chess, said it was all about planning and staying one jump ahead. But mostly it was slaughter, my pawns going down quick and then the rest, too. Dad would give me a look just when I was putting a piece down, a look that said you ain't thinking ahead, and I could have pulled it back, but didn't 'cause I didn't have any other ideas what to do.

We painted Glen's room so when he came back he might want to live there for awhile, maybe drive up and back to Fresno to take classes at the J.C. on the G. I. bill. We did the walls and the ceiling in blue and the wood trim around the windows in white. It looked pretty good, if I say so myself, and I was glad to do it, and glad my dad didn't seem to think I was a nuisance. In fact, he gave me one whole wall to myself, and I took my time and tried to do it right.

I thought since everything was blue like the sky we could do some clouds with the white on the ceiling. Glen would maybe like that I said because after all that time out of doors maybe that room would seem kind of small and we wouldn't want him to want go somewhere else, but dad said that would take more art than we had and maybe Glen would

have had enough of the sky and in any case, I was-
n't to worry.

*   *   *   *

Mother was tired that Sunday, but we got her to
go. Pastor Jenson's wife was having the potluck and
raffle she always had come the end of the winter at
First Baptist. They had a pig that they roasted and all
the stuff the women brought, and it wasn't the kind
of thing you could miss without people asking why,
so we went. First Baptist was a big brick and mortar
place that mother said was put up to spite the downtown Catholics. It had two towers that shot up like
the rooks on our chess board and a doorway in
between that pointed up at its center and the doors
must've weighed a ton they were so thick, though
they cut up at their tops at a sharp angle, real cunning, fitting the doorway exact.

People parked all around, cars nosed into the
curbs so if you were late you had to walk a couple of
blocks just to get there. Going in we said hi to everybody, my mom looking worn with little spoons of
dark under her eyes as we clunked down the wood-

en stairs to the basement. There were scads of people down there, everybody moving around putting their stuff down and saying, *How are you?* and *Oh really?* and *I declare*, and such. They had lots of tables and those wicked folding chairs that give your rear a real workout, and up front there was donated stuff for the raffle laid out on a table the size of the Last Supper.

It was so crowded people were elbowing around, though doing it polite. We found my mother a seat, and my dad went off with some of the guys from the plant, out through the back and up behind the church to see about the pig. I had my notebook of birds I was drawing with me as my mother said I might get bored, but I left it on the table and went off myself to check on the prizes. They had a fishing rod and some tackle, a portable Zenith radio, two stainless steel Thermoses, a case of Coca-Colas in those little-kid bottles, a gift certificate for twenty-five dollars you could use at the five and dime, and a set of kitchen knives sticking out of a wooden block. But my eyes got fastened on a vase made of river-green glass that opened up at its top like a fan. I was fascinated by the little bubbles of light trapped in its surface. There was a card set out front of it that told how it was hand-blown in West Virginia, and I knew it was the thing my mother would want in her room for the ancestors, though she'd never admit to that kind of longing.

Sooner or later everybody settled down some, and Pastor Jenson went up front and tapped on this beak of a microphone that topped a metal contraption, thin as a one-legged flamingo and wobbly. I was standing off to the side. I looked for my folks and saw my mother sitting there where we'd left her, sitting by herself, looking clean off into space. My mother could go off by herself whenever she wanted. It was a habit she had. Just let her eyes blank out and take a walk in her mind. *I was just taking a walk* is what she'd say, and she'd smile at me, and I'd feel left out for a moment and a little troubled because I knew there was no way I could go along someplace like that. I could see that the ladies weren't talking to her and so she'd gone walking, and I started over towards her.

I was halfway there when people hushed and Pastor Jenson called over the microphone, that hissed and cracked, for the Almighty to come down to that basement and bless us 'cause we were the faithful, and then he asked that the crooked be made straight, and we all said, *Amen.* Then they carried in the pig, came swinging through the back door with it on a board, four grown men carrying it, plump and shiny and roasted dark as caramel and dripping in the juices it had made itself. I thought that's what people were sighing about, because this sigh, this sound like a dog's low growl coming outside your window at night, coming in soft from way out in a field, this sound like that goes through the room, and I turned and saw it was the Jew coming down the stairs and into that room, my brother's passion poured like pale beer into a long green vase of a dress, laughing softly and looking at him and holding his arm ever so lightly.

*   *   *   *

With the praying done, folks wanted to eat, so they went on and started, the room heating up with plenty of noise, some of the men standing to eat from their plates as it was that crowded. And those two went around, the Jew patting guys on the back, telling jokes, I suppose, because the guys laughed, but you knew they were uncomfortable as they'd move off as soon as they could, and he'd have to go on to the next and start with the jokes and the glad handing again. She didn't say anything, hardly looked around at all, just smiled kind of distracted, keeping her arm on his.

They didn't eat. A Jew won't eat pig, not ever, on account of their part of the Bible. She sipped a little coffee, pinky finger pointing out to show she was class. I got three dollars from my dad and bought tickets so as to be ready for luck if it was coming my way. And you know, I knew I would win that glass vase that day. Luck's like that. It builds up. And sometimes, you feel it when it's about to come down on you. Maybe it was that I was always waiting that put me in that mind. Anyway, Mrs. Webley, the librarian, got the fishing stuff, which everybody knew she'd give to her boy, Arthur, who was thirty-seven and lived at home except when he went hunting for two weeks like he did every winter. Janice Figgs squealed like a little kid when she figured out that she'd won the Zenith, as if she needed it, which she didn't, being rich like she was—her brother owned four liquor stores and was a soft touch for his sister on account she was too ugly for anyone to marry.

Somebody I didn't know got the Coca-Colas, and a girl from high school who wore braces and kept smiling as if it hurt—she'd smile and then suck her lips—got the paper with the twenty-five dollars written on it in a big bold hand in indigo ink and signed by Rudy Shepherd who owned Rudy's Five and Dime and where she could go now for as long as that twenty-five held out. I don't know who got the kitchen knives. The whole time I was waiting, feeling quiet and sure and excited at the same time, so much so that when Pastor Jenson's wife, who had a rump like a Shetland pony, and a round yellow hat that looked like a lemon drop, leaned into the mike to read out the last number, pulling down on her dress that kept riding up, I had already stood up *before* she read out my number, *L278.* Everybody clapped and dad looked surprised, and my mother perked up, astonished and pleased.

I brought it back and put it on the table in front of her, and she was saying, "My, my, it's so pretty, " playing it up because I'd given it to her, but also really taken by its beauty. Uncle Aquilla was sitting two tables over and he nodded at me and my folks. My aunt, sitting next to him, who dyed her hair root beer red and had little pointed teeth like a possum's,

41

smiled politely at my mother, and all was fine, and it didn't bother me then that my brother's passion was there for everybody to see how he had no hold on her, his being gone and all, and I didn't care at all that Uncle Aquilla's eyes were flicking over those two with what I thought was curiosity, but that I see, now, was envy, which some say is the real root of evil.

*   *   *   *

It was the old guys in front of the tire shop who'd told me Glen loved his country in spite of his race. Let me know, too, he had it bad for that woman. That's how I knew for sure he'd had knowledge of her before he went over the seas and before he came back and showed his desire for everyone to see. *How's your brother's passion?* is what one of them had said, winking at the others who'd all laughed and enjoyed it, admiring their deftness, all laughing like congratulations and thank-you to one another's cunning. I guess I laughed, too, to please them, to show I was worldly, and I admit I felt a little shame, yet the truth is that what they'd said gave me some hope that maybe Glen would stick around so as to be near her when he came home, which I hoped would be soon, and it's part of what made me go by where she lived once I knew where that was.

Mary Ann Sheeney had the very smallest house you would ever see. Didn't have more than three rooms if you counted the bathroom. Just a bedroom with an old iron bed and some red and beige drapes sewn up out of paisley sheets and a little lamp with a ruby shade made of glass. There was just a little bathroom and the rest was a living room of sorts with a kitchen along one wall, a gas stove in one corner, a refrigerator the size of a dryer, a little table for eating. It had a wood burning stove against one wall, and in the center of the room was a couch with its back, humped up like a camel, and that's all. I could see in if I wanted by creeping up close and looking right through those sheets on account they were thin, though I did that only once.

Usually, I came out of the ditch and lay up near an old oak in the tall grass on my belly. Somebody had recently whitewashed the place and there were geraniums spotting the beds red out back of the porch. You could see under the paint the wood was old. It was a place that had been there a long while, probably before most. Out back and to the left of where I usually watched, there was a little barn, a bit bigger than the house, with double doors and a weather vane, a rusty rooster on top that squealed if there was any wind. She parked her car in there, a Chevy Impala with the front panels grayed with primer.

There was a dirt lane that ran right up out front and there was grass all around. There was a grove of pecans on one side, the ditch on the other, and beyond that were couple of acres of blackberries, very juicy when they swelled in summer, fat as bumblebees.

From where I lay, I could only see the back side of the house. It was cool in the grass in the shade of that tree and sometimes I'd drift off and maybe sleep a little. That day the blackberries weren't out but the grass was lime green and so fresh it must have already been spring. I was stretched out and thinking, chewing a long blade of sourgrass, sucking the juice from it and practicing my spit which was good, but nowhere near what the old guys downtown could do. I thought no one was home because the stereo wasn't playing. My brother's passion played stuff I never heard at home or on my station. She liked this dreamy stuff with saxophones and basses wandering around, climbing up and down with minds of their own and a lady singing husky and alone.

I was watching a blue jay sling itself down over a big calico Tom, strafing it with a sharp *scree, scree, scree* until that Tom shot across the lot and slipped under the house. I had my notebook, and I thought maybe I should try doing a bird like that, on the wing, not just sitting still like I usually did.

But the shouting started, and it went straight quick to screaming. It was her screaming, harsh and high and angry, but it ended up fearful and surprised. I shot to my feet when I heard it, got up without thinking, forgetting myself, forgetting I had no business being there and no business knowing about things the way I did. I stood up, ready to run, but my legs wouldn't go. Stood up in plain sight next to that tree, stood still as that tree when she came out the back door, the screen door flying open and banging, her falling back off the step the way I would if I was horsing around at the municipal pool.

But there was no water there to catch her, only the earth, and she went down to it hard, hard enough I thought I heard the breath push out of her though that couldn't be true as I was too far away. She stood up, wobbly as a colt, with that water-light that comes with spring wavering round her, the back of her hand to her mouth and her head down, hair falling forward from the top of her head.

Then he came out and dropped down the step and swung down on her, fist closed as if hitting a man, punching her head so she dropped with no sound, just folded up and collapsed under the blow to lay there on her side, not moving at all. And he stood over her, and then he seemed to remember to look around. I couldn't see his eyes, but his head darted back and forth and then pointed off across the ditch toward the blackberries planted in rows, heat waves, squiggly above them.

My heart was thumping, big jack-rabbit thumps, but I didn't move and I realized he didn't see me, he was looking right through me and beyond, and I thought I must look like a stump at that distance or a shoot coming off that tree, and I was glad I was too troubled to move.

He went down on his knees and slipped his arms through his suspenders and unbuttoned his jeans and his back side showed pale and naked and private as anything could that's not used to the light, and he pushed up her dress and rolled her over on her belly. And he went at her, the desire in him fierce, struggling and huffing, trying to get free, his head up and watching the sky, I guess, head up like he's listening hard for some sound that's up there that's too rare to hear, like maybe those whistles they have pitched high for animals, some sound I don't know directly.

I don't think he ever heard it either, no matter how much he wanted, 'cause he stopped with a jerk and his whole self went stiff, and then he surprised me and gave me more confusion than I knew what to do with. He started crying to himself in ugly little sobs. Like he was suddenly a baby with his backside no longer a secret, out there ridiculous and bumpy. He was sniffling and wiping his eyes and buttoning himself up in a hurry, fumbling fast as he could, and he didn't even look at her except once quick when he pulled back her hair to see her face for a second. Then he ran around the front of the house, shirttails flying, stumbling out of sight, and I heard a truck firing up and the tires get hold and it rumbling away, the gears climbing off in the distance.

And then I knew she and I were connected 'cause I felt the wind rushing out of us both, and the sun, coming all that way through space, pressing its thumbs to us, pushing into our eyes, making everything black and orange, and I realized I'd closed my eyes so I opened them, and I knew she was alive even though I could see she was lying there limp, and I saw, too, plainly, that Uncle Aquilla had left his hat, a P.F. Stanley & Co. cap, blue and yellow the way they all are, and I saw for sure into the future when I'd have no answer when at dinner my dad would stick out his chin and arrow his eyes down on me as usual, pretending his displeasure, saying, *Well, how was your day?*

*   *   *   *

My idea was that I was connected to my brother 'cause he was tied to his passion in some way, sure as if he was sewn tight with threads thinner than hair. So it was that I was tied, too, and that caused my shame. I was ashamed I ran off like I did. Ran straight out through the orchard and across the fields, not even bothering going back down in the ditch. Ran hard as I could with that music of hers playing loud in my ears, that woman crying about her man and his ways that were all trouble, and I knew I was now something like that man who was no good, on account he ran off and left her to make that music, pitiful and blue.

47

Also it was a shame I didn't tell what I knew. I wanted to think she'd brought it on herself, that her trouble was hers. If I told my dad, it would be his, sure enough, and that didn't seem fair. But I felt marked then. I'd lived up to everything Pastor Jenson said about those who would deny the Lord same as Peter, so I knew I wasn't even with the world, and I'd have to look out for a chance to right things if I could.

I don't know how I knew she wouldn't talk, but I did. I didn't go by there for awhile, and it was some while till I saw her again. It was downtown in the drugstore when I spotted her from the end of an aisle. She had big dark glasses on that made her head look like a beautiful insect of some kind, maybe a butterfly, though her face was still bruised and a little yellow on one side and she looked older somehow. She was wearing a pair of cutoffs, hemmed in pink, and a blue blouse, hair braided in a little rope that went round the top of her head.

But what made me feel bad was I saw that when she walked she was doing it carefully, trying to hide a little limp that she had. I wondered if that would be forever or if it would heal up in its time. I was thinking about turning the other cheek and wondering what profit there could be in that, and I was thinking about vengeance, and feeling the shame on me hard because I knew I hadn't done anything and it wasn't likely I could.

And she was coming down the aisle slowly and spotted me watching her and she looked over the tops of her glasses to see me clearly. Her eyes looked frightened, though that passed so fast into kindness that it was almost as if I hadn't seen the fear at all, and she smiled. Soft sunshine making me feel both whole and lost at the same time.

*   *   *   *

What's the matter? my mother would ask. She went on asking that for a week, though I told her nothing, nothing was wrong. One day when she was not working, and my father had gone over to help Uncle Aquilla pour cement for his patio, I was lying on the living room floor reading the comics when she called to me from her room. I went down the hall to the back of the house where my folks had their spot. She was sitting up in bed and motioned me to her. She was petting my head when she asked again what was the matter. And this time I said the truth, or part of it, anyway.

"I saw Glen's passion," I said. That set her to thinking the way that I knew it would. Her eyebrows knitted up, though she was careful to act like nothing unusual.

Finally, she says, "Where?" So I knew she was-

49

n't going to pretend he didn't have one.

"Her house," I said, letting it go at that.

She threw back her covers and got up, her back to me because she was only wearing a nightgown, and went to the closet for her robe. She put it on and came back to me, took my hand and walked me to her parlor where she took one of those matches, long as a pencil, and scratched it against the brick of the fireplace; and then, carefully, she touched one of the candles on the mantelpiece awake. She ran her fingers over the names on one of those tablets, squeezing my hand when she did that.

"Sit," she said and I did, and then she went to a drawer in the sideboard and took out a paper with a picture of a blanket drawn on it which she showed me before she placed it in a dish and took the candle and lit it. "I'm cold today. I don't know why that should be. Your grandmother was like that, always cold." But I already knew the picture of the blanket that was burning then was supposed to keep grandmother warm wherever she was.

Mother closed her eyes and went walking, I guess, and I knew I was supposed to stay quiet and wait, but I didn't want to and I said, "There's a lot that have a passion for her." And my mother's eyes opened and slid sideways so as to study me good.

"Perhaps that's her nature," she said, almost gentle.

I think *perhaps* has a curious meaning of its own that she wasn't telling, but I said, "Why?" I knew I was being stubborn, but my father wasn't there and so I was being wise, taking a chance.

"Of course, it's possible it is not her nature and if so..."

50

"Why would that be her nature?"

"...then she will suffer. *"

"It's not, it's not her nature," I said, 'cause I knew about the suffering.

"I know what my father would say to you right now: 'Stretch a bow to its full and you will wish you had stopped in time.' "

And I was seeing the sunlight tipping the grass out back of her place, that field gone to fire...

"It's her business, Dave."

...and the struggling and the blue jays screaming from the trees, the sky pulled tight, and the bow that she was, stretched to its full. I didn't want to know anymore then. My mother was watching me carefully. She leaned close and pulled me to her, her cheek against mine, her eyelashes brushing my skin like I was her baby again. "You stay away from there," she whispered.

And I let it go. I didn't say, *Why?* anymore, because, in my way, I knew.

*   *   *   *

The Nam made a hole in my brother's ear, made
a hole in the little drum that's in there. Sound bust-
ed through and did it, punched it out. *Had to call our
own artillery in,* he was saying on the phone. I heard
it ringing and I picked it up because I was the only
one home. *That's all we could do, Dave* is what he
was telling, how he and some he was with got their
position run over one night. *That's my luck,* he said
and I knew he meant the good kind because he told
how all of those others' luck was the worst kind.

Uncle Sam couldn't use him without his having
both of his ears working. He said he put it all in a letter a couple of weeks back. *We never got that,* was
all that I said. He said some more, stuff about
Okinawa and the hospital there, how he was pretty
much as good as new, and that he was free.

*Tell them that, Dave. I'm free to come home and
I will be. Soon.*

OK, I said and then the line got fouled up with a
sound like wasps crawling around, bunched up and
crazy, and then that got faint as if they took off and
were moving away and then the line, it went dead. I
hung up the phone then, and sat down in the big soft
velvet chair that's there by the front door where the
phone sits, sat there, my feet not touching the

ground. I was thinking how dumb I was not even telling Glen I was glad he was OK and coming right back, and I was thinking about what it would feel like to have your friends all dead and what it would be like to have your ear opened up like a window torn open in a storm, bits of leaves and dust and the night blowing in. So I just sat there waiting for someone to come home so I could ask about that.

*   *   *   *

In a small town, you do something and it is a pretty sure bet that somebody will know it, so those scabs played a dangerous game. It wasn't just crossing the picket line that was a danger. People knew where you lived. Those scabs would load up a car, pack themselves in for courage, and then drive fast as they could through the gate at P.F. Stanley and Company. Work at the plant took time to learn so it wasn't as if those scabs could do much, but it was the sight of them that made people sore. If it weren't for Erin Bleacher those scabs would've got killed.

Erin Bleacher shot animal hormones into his own body. Every part of him grew, except his head which stayed the same and made him look like a potato in a t-shirt with a white melon on top for a head. No neck, fat white arms the size of most men's legs. Some said he was an *Angel* come down by way of Oakland, came down on his Sportster after some of his brains got eaten by crystals of meth which are supposed to be as sure a poison as you can get if you've got that affliction, if you let yourself go like that and get bound up in the flesh.

He was half of him dumb and the other half mean, and that's all there was that I knew of him. They say he killed somebody with a cue stick, once, or so he liked you to think. But they that would tell it were those that were desirous of some attention when they talked, so who knows. They say the cops used him when they needed something done on the side. And it was everybody's knowledge that the old Fresno Hotel took care of his rent as long as he kept the girls there in line, so all that was his were the wages of sin. Still, the old men on the bench were surprised when he started showing up along with some other fellows, strange sorts because they'd grown these Rip Van Winkle beards over their young men's faces, surely ugly enough to be his genuine friends, all of them showing up outside the plant in the mornings to open the gates and wave the scabs through.

Some of those scabs were black boys, *tar babies*, I said to my folks when we were driving one evening out in the country, and my dad reached back without even looking and slapped the side of my head so hard I toppled over in the seat.

Amos, my mother says, *he doesn't know what he's saying.* But I guess I did ever after because I took care not to say it again. Those two were nervous then, what with the strike and with the knowledge that Glen could show up any time.

One morning I saw Erin Bleacher wave those boys in and somebody threw a beer bottle that went head over heels, somersaulting out of the crowd to pop open in bit-size pieces at his feet. And Erin Bleacher pulled a double-barreled shotgun from under his coat, a shotgun sawed-off nearly as short as a pistol and duct-taped on the handle, and he shot it in the air, his hand bouncing twice, those blasts echoing off the two-story buildings clear across the street, sending the pigeons clattering from the rooftops there. The men backed away so the scabs could go through; and across, down the street, the cops in their car just sat there minding the business they wanted to mind and no more.

That same day, right after Erin Bleacher locked up the gates, Uncle Aquilla came out to the fence and tried talking to the men. He came out slowly with his thumbs in his suspenders and chewing a cigar into one corner of his mouth. He stood at the chain link and unhooked his thumbs to raise his arms as if he's surrendering, but he's not, he's just curling his fingers through the fence and resting against it. "Men," he hollered. "Men," he hollered again, even louder, though the men had already shut up and were only a few feet from him, on their side of the fence, waiting on what he's got to say.

"Don't you be fooled by this ...this outside agitation," he said, quieter now 'cause he sees the men are hushed and because he'd got his nerve up. "What does this joker from Seattle or wherever the hell he claims he's from got to do with our work here? Huh? NOTHING!" He looked around, studying faces. "That's right, nothing. I'm saying to you boys, don't kill this company. Don't do it." He shook his head, and you could tell there was some actual sorrow there in his voice and some fear, too.

And the men were silent and that particular day the old guys on the bench were holding their tongues, and I looked round, but didn't see the Jew anyplace. And then I saw my dad. He was back some, in among the men, wearing his khakis and a red flannel shirt and his old blue and white nylon Nascar windbreaker. And he had a P. F. Stanley cap on. I watched him. I could tell he was thinking because he was biting at the inside of his cheek the way he'd do before he'd make a move on the chessboard at home, chewing like that on the inside of his mouth before he'd pick up a knight and go forward and flank to the side, part of the plan, staying one jump ahead.

He snatched his hat off his head and flung it out over the fence where Uncle Aquilla, surprised, studied it on the ground where it landed, until the men began to laugh—started chuckling and then laughing full-out—and somebody did a hoop and holler, and they all started taking off their caps and sailing them over the fence, those caps flying clumsy as chickens with their wings clipped. And Uncle Aquilla turned around and started walking back to the plant and the caps were landing, rolling at his

heels and his backside is all we saw, and I was thinking it don't look much better for being covered up,
the fat and the wrinkles covered up, walking away
like that, dangerous and shamed.

*   *   *   *

I was lying up there in the weeds, waiting on her
to come on home from wherever she'd gone, the one
time I talked to him myself. I was looking out across
the fields, kind of humming to myself, bored, watching this skinny white crane, like one I'd seen in my
library book, saw it off just a few yards away. It was
jumping round in the grass like a Chinese kite and
trying to take off, and I was thinking, *No wind*, until
I see it was because it had one of its wings broke and
that was why. I wanted to help, wanted to sneak up
and capture it and take good care of it until it could
mend. But I already knew touching a wild thing
would most likely kill it, and besides it was too big
for me to even know how I could get hold of it proper and get it home.

It wasn't making any sound, just hopping in circles on its long orange legs and beating the one good

57

wing and trying to make the other one go but just making it worse—bent and crazy, snapping softly in the wind like hung laundry. It didn't cry or make any sound, its eyes, black buttons, shining with pain, and I realized it would never get out of there, some dog or something would get at it, or it'd starve. And when I figured that out it felt like the first time of something, felt like a finger pushing slow and hard into my heart, and I didn't like it at all, didn't like that I saw that's just how it is sometimes.

I wasn't sure, then, anymore about shooting birds all the time, that in the future, I should put more thought on that. Soon enough, it ran off down the edge of that field, scuttled away, me watching after it some. And I settled back in, got to feeling lazy, just watching the clouds, and fell asleep, dead-out with no dreams, just black and nothing, limbs heavy as logs.

When I woke up, right off I saw that somebody had to have been sitting next to me while I slept, sitting there long enough to smoke three Pall Mall non-filter cigarettes and then stub them out on the ground right next to me.

I looked around. There was only her little white house and the oak trees and the grass and the sky still wobbling overhead, fly-specked and so rich you could swim in it, almost. Then the hairs on the back of my neck stood up, and I turned round and there was the Jew sitting on a long branch in the tree, right next to me. I jumped up. "Lord," I said before I knew I was going to say it, "you gave me a scare."

He just smiled and swung his legs back and forth

very slowly and gave me a kind of salute with a long-necked bottle of beer he had in one hand. He was only a few feet up in that tree, up on the first good branch, and he was just taking the day anyway that it came, I could see that, just relaxing, but still, I tell you, to me, right then, it was as if he'd dropped out of the sky, trouble sitting there as close as your shoulder, sudden and real. I said that. "You're the one that's trouble." And he laughed a little, silently to himself, appreciating what I'd said in some way of his own.

I suppose, he said, though he didn't say it, it's just what he meant, I could tell, when he nodded and lifted his shoulders. Then he took a long pull on that beer, head tilted back, but those big black eyes of his on me still. That's when I noticed his hair was wavy and a bit long, and I thought, maybe, I might like to look that way myself when I was grown.

Then he said to me, "She's not home, bub," the insides of his eyes all prickly with stars, crinkled with humor. I didn't say anything. But I felt the shame on me hard, burning my ears. I just stood there to see what was going to happen next. I figured he could make some sport of me if he cared to as it was true I'd been keeping track of things, and he knew then. I stood there so he understood I was not denying anything, but I wasn't sorry, either.

"She's not your passion, is she?" I blurted out, but it didn't sound like a question.

His face went dark for a second or two like a shadow of a cloud slipping over some flat, sunny field. "No...not really a passion," he said.

I shook my head, my head saying yes, that's what I thought, then I couldn't help myself and I said, "She's my brother's."

And our eyes met and held on and he said, "Who's your brother?'"

"He's Glen. He's gone to the Nam."

"Oh..." he said. Then he jumped down out of the tree, and stared off into the fields and there was sun spotlighting them so hard they looked bleached, and he wound up and tossed the beer bottle out as far as he could and watched after it where it went down, *thud*, in the grass. He was looking off that way when he said, "Well, you don't worry. I won't be around here long."

"He's supposed to be back sometime soon," I added, because I thought he should know it and I didn't care if I was sounding bold.

He looked at me, one side of his face hunkered down, half-sad, half-smirk.

He took out a handkerchief from his pocket and shook it loose like a sudden white blossom and wiped the dirt off his shoes, forgetting me, full of care for his shoes, kind of weird. I didn't know what to make of that and looked down at my own shoes and started thinking it's time I got going. I guess he was uncomfortable and why not as I'd said what I did. So I turned and I left, and I believed that was because I'd had enough for that day, what with that white bird still spinning round in the grass and him they called trouble in a tree, that I'd gone then and talked to, making claims for my brother.

*   *   *   *

Mother grew lemon grass back of our house. She said it was as good as they grew in the old country. She was forever chopping it up and mixing it in with chicken or peas or whatever she wanted. In the ground it looked like the stalks of green onions, though it could grow taller than me. Cats would lie up in there and go half-mad with the pleasure. It was all mystery to me why they liked it. Sometimes they'd spring up out of there, full of the wild and impressed with themselves, enjoying their spunk and the way they'd surprised you.

She had peppers and tomatoes and squash and *whatnot* growing in summer. For a long time my mother had pestered my dad to build her a square box out of redwood so she could keep leaves and garbage and such so as to have something to use to nourish her garden. The box was to have no bottom and the top would be covered with a tin lid with holes poked through. She called it a cooker because it was supposed to heat up and cook down all the stuff into food for the vegetables. I liked the idea. Sun and the closed-up box warming the stuff, breaking it down, but the stuff still there, just changed and ready to change again when we'd rake it into the vegetable garden so the roots of the plants could

61

clutch it, hold it, and take it up into themselves. Things really could go round forever.

Of course, I never saw it until my brother built it for her the first week he was back. Yes, that was a week to remember. Glen was always a natural carpenter. And believe it, he was out there early, one of those first days it was hot, him not wearing a shirt, first thing in the morning, the day after he showed up, his hammer going down, the nails yelping hard as he punched them into the lumber my dad had bought for the job over a year before. Mother was in the bathroom crying out of relief or maybe sorrow of some kind, and my dad was out there hovering around, nodding and handing Glen stuff, neither of them talking. It looked from my window as if my dad couldn't help himself being a pest. He was pretending he was watching the job, but it was plain he was just watching Glen, drinking him up with his eyes that were weak with that kind of thirsty.

Even from my window I could tell Glen wasn't himself. I mean he was himself, he was Glen, and he was my brother and he was glad to see us, but we made him nervous in some way we hadn't before. Even that day you could tell he wished my dad would go into the house and leave him be to let himself go in that work, and I believe dad knew that himself, but couldn't bring himself to be quit of his son.

I'd had enough sense to stay out of the way, just shook his hand when he showed up at the door the day before, spiffed out in his dress uniform, his hair cropped as short on the sides as a Plains Indian, those I'd seen in a book, the ear on his left side plastered over neatly with some kind of putty, his eyes like almonds damp with some rain but already drying, his cheeks sharp, and his shoulders new with muscles. He came into the house and put his arm on my shoulder, let it rest there the whole time he said hello to my folks, well hello and hello son and hello mom and everybody hello and everyone stiff and shaky, bound up and relieved at the same time and his hand staying there on my shoulder, like I was holding him up, my brother, Glen.

And that's how it was at first with both of them, my mother and my dad watching him, trying to see who he was now, all the time watching him and him knowing that and him patient with them, letting them come closer than he'd like with their eyes, which they did all the time, sometimes secretly, sometimes not, sometimes them just staring at him at the dinner table until he'd look at them and smile a very little smile, patient with them, not wanting to show them directly, but letting them see for themselves, waiting for them to see that yes, he was, yes, all of him, changed.

So that was June, and I didn't have any school to bother with. I was free to do pretty much as I pleased. The ditches were running, heavy and smooth, filled to the brim, that water the color of thick green tea, the surface flat and untroubled, which was a deception because that water was pulling fast to be sure. Not all the ditches ran at the same time. Some were empty; then you might go by on another day and there they were full. That was a time to take care about being down there. They kept that water moving all over the place on account it was hot and the earth was thirsty and there had to be water now here and then there and all over.

I still had choir practice on Thursdays at First Baptist in the afternoon, but that wasn't much so I decided I'd get a paper route. I could make fifty dollars in a Month, the guy told me when I signed on, that is, if I was careful not to be wasteful and if I could be quick and steady with my time—which I could. Turned out *The County Guide* was quick and regular themselves. You got charged for every paper. Everything was written down in a book and come the end of the month you owed them whether your customer paid up or not. Somebody moved away and didn't pay, well, that was your pocket that got picked, not *The Guide's*. Quick and steady—you paid them no matter. Still, I had plenty of time to keep an eye on Glen, which is what I wanted to do most and I did. He liked the way we'd painted his room and had said, *And you picked the colors, Dave?* Though he knew that I did because we'd told him. I knew he was just making a fuss to show he appreciated it 'cause his happiness was more studied than not. *And you painted some, too?* And I'd smile in spite of myself, proud and red in the ears and foolish, his words like a hand petting me down.

He was sleeping up there in his room again and working around the house and working odd jobs when he could, though at that time with the men out of the plant people did their own odd jobs and weren't paying for that. He drove up to the VA hospital sometimes. I don't know why that was a secret, why nobody talked about it when I was around, though I'd overheard him asking to take the van up to Fresno to see the doctor. Wasn't long he didn't have that stuff covering up his ear anymore. He looked normal.

One night sometime after he was back, I was at the kitchen table working in my notebook on a drawing I'd started maybe a few weeks earlier. I'd copied it out of my book with pencil, and I was trying to get it right using colors I'd found in the basement, ones my mother had used when she'd taken a class, these oily professional crayons. I was making a Paradise flycatcher. I'd wanted it the same red its body had in the book, like cayenne pepper, and I'd had some fierce trouble with that, though the match wasn't bad. I was filling in the head and the long, long tail feathers with black when Glen came in and sat down to watch me. It was hot, being summer, and he wiped his forehead carefully with a dishtowel and slurped on the glass of iced tea he had with him. He lit a cigarette and let a little ball of blue smoke roll up just outside his mouth before he pulled it in and down in his lungs, his face a little sigh of pleasure. "Never saw one like that," he said, meaning my work.

I looked at him. His hair was starting to come in, nubs of lead gray, just like the points of pencils. He had on a blue t-shirt and old Levis, soft from the wash, and he was more relaxed than I'd seen him, but not much. I wondered if he hadn't been round to his passion's or if he'd forgotten her.

"Over there you saw mostly chickens, unless you were on patrol out somewhere in the trees. That's where you had to go to see ones like that," he said nodding toward my Paradise bird. "Those kind, the colorful ones, they stick to the canopy, the tops of the trees and you only hear them. Then, once in awhile, all of a sudden, a whole flock of one kind will zip by, their wings flashing, and then they're gone. You have to look quick." Then his eyes went up, tracing the kitchen ceiling, following those birds off into the distance, one eye squinting some as if it pained him. And he wasn't there in the kitchen any-more, he'd flown off thousands of miles and it gave me a chill, because I saw then that's what he wanted and there wouldn't be any stopping him, whether he wanted to or not, as he wouldn't be looking back once he went, not even for me.

So I did something foolish, said, "Don't you want to see that MaryAnn Sheeney?"

His head came back down, and his eyes climbed back down, and he looked at me steady, but didn't say anything. His face relaxed blank as a tablet of stone, his eyes cooling off like little gas jets turned down low, getting even more narrow than God'd made them. He pulled on his smoke and his fingers were shaky, just a hair shaky, and he swallowed the smoke down and spewed it up, twisting and blue. I was looking at the tiny beads of sweat on his upper lip when he spoke. "Come again?" he said, turning his good ear toward me, though I knew he'd heard me just fine.

"The red-headed woman. The one that lives down by the ditch in that little white house." I guess fear made me cunning and also a danger and I should have stopped right then. I should've been struck dumb on the spot.

He didn't speak then. And I went back to my painting, afraid of myself. I was screwing the tail feathers up, making them too fat, my lines nervous and splotchy. He pushed back his chair, it scraping the linoleum, and went over to the sink to run the water on his cigarette and drop it in the trash. He was looking out the kitchen window, though it was so black it was a mirror, and he said very softly, "You know there's a bird that stays in the air all summer?" He was looking at himself in the window. "Imagine that."

67

"What?" I said.

"Henley... he's a guy, sort of bird nut, I knew in the service. He was stationed in Europe for awhile; he said the Air Force tracked them on radar. He said they would circle in the evenings over this big reservoir that was out back of the base and then rise upwards at dusk. They'd just keep climbing and stay aloft all night. And get this, he said in the summer they never touched down at all." The thought of it had him thinking, his head cocked like a dog that's asking for an answer.

"Never touched down at all," I repeated after him.

"That's something, isn't it, Dave?" he said, not turning around, still looking at his face in the window.

"How they eat?" I said.

"Catch their dinner on the wind. Get their water that way too, from the bodies of insects."

"What do they call those birds?" I asked.

"Pretty sure he said it was a swift. Common swift. That was probably it. That's a small bird, heart the size of a pea, I'd bet."

"Size of a pea," I repeated, my mouth hanging open, keen with the wonder.

He turned around from the sink and he looked at me. Then slowly he smiled, kind of weary, and said, "Don't be in such a hurry to grow up, Dave."

Course, that was lost on me, coming, as it did, too late.

Summer is hard in the San Joaquin Valley. The sky loses its blue and goes white, the red in the glass thermometer that my dad had tacked up on the porch, then, would slip up above a hundred and the middle of most days the shadows are sucked up, shriveled thin. There's no wind at all, except in the evenings when it finally kicks up with soft sweet smells of the grass and the raisins and such. You'd think folks would slow down in that weather, but they don't. They work harder than ever, especially out on the farms.

Summer's when the men at the plant got the idea of a food bank. They started going out in trucks after a farmer had harvested his tomatoes or asparagus or whatever and they'd comb through the fields and get what was left. They boxed it up so people could come pick it up at First Baptist. *Times are lean*, is what people said and folks were feeling it, I guess. Two guys got in a fist fight right there in the hall at the church over a box of cucumbers until my dad broke it up. He split one fellow's lip, who looked more surprised than hurt, his mouth hanging open, a spider of blood dangling wet from his teeth.

The men still hung around outside the plant every day except now they took it in turns. Maybe twenty or thirty at a time. Some found work picking in the fields, but not many as it was work they didn't know well enough to do fast and fast is the only way you could make any money at all doing that sort of thing. And pruning and spraying and irrigating and such was a skill of its own. No farmer wanted to train them if they were just going to leave once the strike broke.

Lots of those boys got drunk. I know because the bars on Front Street were on my route. I was supposed to just drop the paper on the sidewalk outside, but I always got off my bike and went in to leave the paper right there on the bar. Nobody told me to do that. I just wanted to and figured I could. I wanted to know about the insides of those places.

I would walk right in, push open those doors that were upholstered like the seats of an automobile and feel the cool of the place right away. Dark and cool explained why those guys hung around in there. Of course, there was the beer, but I knew that could be had cheaper at the grocery. I never tasted beer myself as my dad had put liquor behind him and made me swear I'd never taste it while I lived in his house, and I was good to my word and never did.

One day I was riding down the sidewalk downtown about to cross the alley next to Jack's Place and Erin Bleacher pulled up in a yellow Pontiac Firebird. He had some brand of ugly on his face and this plump girl with fuzzy hair and a gap in her teeth sitting next to him, giving off this phony smile as best she could.

That Pontiac was rumbling and snorting enough

to shake bolts loose and Erin Bleacher motioned me over to him. I didn't get off of my bike. I just hopped down from the seat, and straddling it, walked it and myself to the curb.

"Hey, squirt," he said. I was looking at his face, seeing it close for the first time. He must have had pimples bad when he was a kid as it looked all pitted and scarred like as if at one time he'd been hit with bird shot pointblank. He had bug eyes sitting out on the ledges of the holes where they were supposed to go. One of his big arms was slung out the window and hanging down along the door of the car like a side of meat.

"Whadda ya hear?" he said.

"Nothing," I said, squinting from the sun.

He smiled real big and I saw one of his eye teeth was gray and going black.

"That Jew in there?"

I looked over at Jack's and then back. "Don't know," I said.

"You know who I mean? The one with the hot-shot shoes. Mr. Bigmouth."

I just looked at him, dumb.

"You taking the paper in?" he said.

"No. Just drop it out front."

"Oh," he said, "that his car?" he pointed to a dented Ford Falcon parked across the street.

"Don't know."

"Why don't you go on in there and tell him I want to talk to him. Tell him I just want to talk to him by himself. Right out here on the sidewalk. Tell him there's plenty of people around. Tell him it's just to talk." He said it like he knew I was going to do it. That made me mad, but I parked my bike anyway and grabbed a paper and went in and walked straight to the bar and left it there. The guy behind the bar asked me, "Kid, you want a Coke?"

I just shook my head and looked around and I saw the guys smoking and playing cards, some of them quiet and sullen, some of them loud, and over by one wall, he was there leaning over the jukebox, smoking. Thin, twin plumes of smoke streaming out of his nostrils. I thought I could tell them Erin Bleacher's outside as I knew each of them hated him and there's plenty of them, but I kept my tongue still.

I quit my watching and walked back toward the bathroom, but then cut around the end of the bar and slipped into the kitchen and out the back door. I just left my bike there. Somebody must've stolen it as it wasn't there next morning when I checked, and those papers, the ones I still had left to deliver, never got out. I had to walk my route after that. But I guess I found out I wasn't no scab, and I had my own work in this world and Erin Bleacher had his and he'd have to do it himself.

*   *   *   *

I didn't even say anything to those old ones out front when we walked right into Nelson's Hardware. Glen sort of nodded at one of them, Mr. Garland, his shop teacher from long time ago. We went directly over to the glass counter where Allen Nelson, Mr. Nelson's overweight, forty-year-old son, was standing in his shirt sleeves with his flabby arms showing and his little red bow tie. He recognized Glen and perked up his black, bushy eyebrows and said, "It came in yesterday." Then he disappeared into the back, and I looked up at Glen, and he knew I was looking at him, but he wouldn't let on while we waited, but his eyes swung down once, those eyes of his dark and shiny as the coffee beans my teacher once showed to my class. They were shiny with pleasure, way they used to be all the time.

I was looking up at him, and I remembered when I was really little and Glen was a kid and it snowed. The only time on record they said it snowed, and Glen woke me up and got me dressed, piled on two sweaters, a scarf, a hat and some mittens, and zippered up my jacket so tight, me so swollen, I could hardly move. Then he took my hand and led me outside and all round our place, holding my hand because I was that small and might fall and showing me everything like he'd stayed up all night himself to make it for me. I cried when I first saw it, everything white, the whole world erased, the air hushed and hurting my cheeks. But he just laughed and showed me it was OK. Sat down in it and rolled over and then jumped up and laughed like a monkey dusted with flour. And I shined with the wonder of him, all that he knew, and I forgot to be scared.

Allen Nelson came out and placed a long white cardboard box on the counter. It had Remington stamped on it in red letters and then I knew. Glen asked for two boxes of shells and then paid him twenty-nine dollars and ninety-four cents and signed some papers and we left. I carried the box that had a nice weight to it, and I just sailed past those old ones out front, though I know they wanted bad to see what we had and were hungry to make some conjecture.

Driving out towards the country, the van wound out loud like a bucket of bolts spun in a dryer, Glen telling how it was all mine but that I wasn't to shoot it unless he was around. He was enjoying the telling, and me too, his voice easy and low. We pulled off the two-lane and took a dirt road out into a vineyard and after awhile of bumping along, we stopped and got out.

It was a one-shot bolt action .22 with a mahogany stock. Glen showed me how to drop the shell in and snap the bolt down. I already knew how to shoot from my pellet gun, but Glen went through it all anyway. How to breathe slow and squeeze off the rounds gentle. He said a single shot was the best because it made you slow down and think what you were doing, how a gun was like all things important, and you had to learn patience and respect for the power that it was.

I shot up both those boxes we had, taking my time, shooting down into a dried-out slough at some piles of old grape stakes that were stacked there for burning, the rounds kicking up little bursts of splintery dust where they went in, Glen nodding when he thought I'd done it right. He wouldn't shoot when I offered, said, "Not today," that faraway look he'd had lots of times since he'd been home climbing back over his face, and I wished I hadn't asked him.

Driving back we went a different way, me knowing why and not saying. The wind seemed to be out of his sail, and he was just watching the road and his driving. He caught me looking glum, which I suppose I did look, so he socked my arm, soft, and smiled in the old way, but then went on back to his own special quiet, his own type of worry, and I felt alone and just counted the mailboxes that were sunk every so often out along the road, and when we passed by her place, I saw him look off up that way, and I looked, too, and that Ford Falcon was parked up there in the grass, and I knew that was no comfort to either of us, that we weren't kids anymore, though we'd tried.

* * * *

There were some said she left because she'd got *preg nut*. That's how they said it. Anyway, that's what I heard. But I know different. I mean, later, I found out myself it was true she was going to have a baby, but that's not why she left. Some said it was 'cause all the trouble the police gave her about the Jew after he was dead. Some said it was because she couldn't bear to be near where my brother had lived. Some said she should have never been let to leave, said, *Bitches in heat ought to be locked up*. I never thought that, but that was their wisdom, and like most of the stuff people think and repeat, it was just everyday ignorance going round and round as it will.

I didn't give much thought to it, as by summer, I was set to working on my own life, my drawing, and my route and the part that gave me some genuine solace, the choir. Mr. Cobley was working us hard for our fall concert. Over and over we practiced those songs, some of them hymns, some of them just ones he thought would go over well. Everything from *This Land Is My Land* to *The Old Rugged Cross*. I was no talent, but I had a good enough ear and could stay with my part and never got whacked around the ears with Cobley's baton which is something he'd do time to time, especially if the practice went long. When that happened he'd start to get sweaty and nervous. More and more he'd tug at his collar and rake his hair with his fingers, and then you knew you'd better not falter because somebody's ears were going to sting.

Actually, I liked him. He was partial to laughing and crying and was an entertainment unto himself. He was what most would call strange in particular. Sometimes, he wore a red jacket, dark as blood, made out of velvet and a white silk tie with a big showy knot the size of a fist. His teeth were yellowed from tobacco and his hands had fingers as long as wax candles with the nails filed down very pretty.

He was a large man, a fact that was set off by the short, quiet one that was usually with him. *Young Mr. Perch,* as Mr. Cobley would say to that one when he wanted to make some change in what was to be played on the piano. Young Perch was as quiet as Mr. Cobley was loud. Young Perch dressed in gray flannel pants and white shirts, black penny loafers and a gray sweater vest he wore even in summer. He hardly spoke or even smiled. Just went along on the piano, his eyes soft, kind of mournful and watchful for Mr. Cobley.

I'd seen them driving around in Mr. Cobley's old Thunderbird sometimes, and I was glad those two had found some friendship, and I thought maybe Mr. Cobley might give up the sauce and come to First Baptist, not just with the choir, but with a pure heart, prepared for Jesus. Though I have to say, I liked him pretty much the way he was. He called us all manner of things—*urchin* and *warbler* and *star dust* and *little apple*. He'd grab our heads with his hands if we'd done well and kiss our foreheads and clap his hands with delight so much that we felt some of that ourselves and were proud. And even if the time was getting late and he was hurting for his weakness and you got clipped, he'd get teary after and say, *Now sugar, I'm sorry.* There's a fondness that's easy to have for somebody who is all themselves and Mr. Cobley was that. I think that must have been hard in a town where most folks took satisfaction in being no different than anyone else.

It was one of those Thursday afternoons when practice ran late and it was getting dark and he was warming up to one of his fits when in walked Glen to the back of that room. He walked up very respectful and stood next to Mr. Cobley.

Young Mr. Perch stopped the piano and Mr. Cobley looked round and saw Glen standing there lanky and calm, his eyes burning soft with his thinking that always showed through because Glen was a thinker it was easy to tell. "Sir, we are working. If you wish to sweep up you'll have to come later," said Mr. Cobley.

Glen told him he was there for his brother and pointed at me, and I stepped forward and waved a little with my hand so Mr. Cobley could see it was me that was the brother. Mr. Cobley looked at Glen and at me, and I saw all of a sudden he had the usual confusion, that is, Glen with the Korean eyes and me with the round ones. Glen got it but he didn't act mad, just said, *He's my brother,* which were words I liked hearing him say. Mr. Cobley sniffed and whipped his eyes up and down Glen and said something like go, then go, both of you go, and we did, out the door and down the steps and into Dad's van, the doors slamming one on each side, *chunk, chunk.*

It's when we pulled into the street that I heard the *shishing* and *ahhing* and saw the black boys in the back scrunched down so you couldn't see them through the windows, and I snapped on the dome light and saw it was real blood, thick and pasty, that'd seeped out, already starting to dry, between the fingers that they had clamped over their heads.

*   *   *   *

"Hell's bells," my dad said. "Now we could end up with a war where everybody gets hurt and nobody's right." Glen just looked at him with some kind of hurt and some kind of strange ugly when he said that. We were in the garage and the doors were closed and those black boys were sitting on the ground. Glen had already poured alcohol on one of their heads and was dabbing it then with a towel.

"Jeez, now I'm screwed three ways to Sunday," said my dad, half under his breath but still loud enough we all heard him.

Glen told about how he found those two running away from the pickets, the men chasing them. How there was some that was liquored-up and who got to talking and ended up throwing bricks and glass bottles of gasoline that they'd lit. Threw them at those scabs coming out in their cars at the end of the shift. Then all hell broke loose and there was blood and vengeance and commotion enough to call down Lord Jesus, least that's how it sounded.

Those boys on the cement floor weren't hurt bad, mostly scared as you could see easy enough, both of them on the floor, wobbly and unsure. Dad wouldn't even look at them. He hated a scab more than anything. But, he hated what'd been done to them, too, and right then, hated those that had done it. *Stupid sons of bitches*, he'd say over and over the next couple of days. *Stupid.*

I wanted to go when Glen drove those black boys back over to their side of town, but I wasn't allowed. I'd been there before. It looked almost the same as some other parts of town except there was cars without wheels in some of the yards and couches out front on the porch. I heard dad say to Glen before he took off that night that he'd better be careful as there was no telling what might be going on over there. The whole place could be burning for all we knew. I thought about that, those couches and those yards and those doorways, dark with those kids hanging in them, all of them rising, all sucked up in the flames,

80

all twisted in fire, all blinded, burned bright, the color of hate.

*   *   *   *

At breakfast the next day, my mom was quiet and my dad looked like he'd beat himself up all the night long. His face was pale and his eyes were bloodshot and he hadn't bothered to shave. Glen said that there was some fair amount of trouble, a few cars over-turned and set afire. And some of the men who were union were locked up. Not for running amok on the colored side of town, but for breaking windows at the plant and obstructing justice, whatever that was. Glen seemed upset in an odd way, polite on the out-side, but as if on the inside, he was sitting on some part of himself he'd had to whip good in some kind of wrestling match. His left cheek would twitch a lit-tle when he talked, and his black eyes didn't want to be there you could tell because they kept dropping away from you and going down to stare at the table.

I was thoughtful that day, and I felt the ditch pulling me, felt I wanted to get out by myself and come up on some other family and watch their lives for a change. I was tired of the fuss and the bother. I didn't start out for her place on purpose, but I suppose I knew that's where I was headed once I climbed down in that ditch. I suppose I knew because it was the only ditch close by that wasn't full and there wasn't too many places other than hers that I could get to by going down that way. Maybe it was on account we were connected that I went. Maybe I wouldn't have gone, if I'd known.

It was bright and fine out and I lingered as I went. Thistle was growing along the banks in bunches of yellow so strong they just jumped at my eyes. I found some pools on the ditch bottom where baby carp were trapped and wiggling around. If the water didn't come again soon their whole world was going to dry up and them too. I tried to think of them getting saved, how the water would come, rushing them off to a slough where they could grow fat as they liked, safe in that water, living easy, rising and falling, slow like big tender blimps. But that was a dream.

That morning the sky was pale hot and no clouds were out, yet when I came down towards her way, came down on her and got close and found her, she was shuddering. Yes, shuddering she was, very much. Her whole self was. She was rocking back and forth on her knees and ever once in awhile a sound would be made, her whole body making that sound, rocking back and forth and letting that sound out. Maybe it was the sound like that litter of kittens that got caught one time when our neighbor was discing his field. He didn't see them in the grass 'till it was too late, and then he shut the tractor down too soon and they were some of them kittens that were only half-dead and wailing. I'd come running over and seen it when he stopped, and he'd made me turn around so as to finish them with a shovel he had on his rig. Said, *Boy you go home. There's nothing to do.* Said, *They're released, now.* Said it gentle.

What I saw plain enough when I came down on her was that that Jew was released. His face was down in a mud puddle and his hands trussed up behind him. And his shoes, still polished, with his feet and his ankles still in them, set up neatly there by his head. I told her that over and over, said, *He's released, now.* But she couldn't seem to find my meaning and just stayed there, down in that ditch, out back of her place, rocking on her knees and shivering in spite of the heat. She leaned forward like she was going to talk to the ground, and I hushed up to listen, but she was just retching some, her insides coming out in filthy brown spurts. Then it was that the flies came down, awkward and light like bits of black ash, fumbly and soft and sticky, and then me it was climbing out of there, running hell bound for help.

*   *   *   *

Chief Horton, dressed in a wrinkled brown suit, and a policeman, in a uniform, came round to see Glen. That was two days after I'd run home and shouted what I knew and Dad called the cops and then got in the van with Glen and took me along to show them where, mother calling after us, *Amos, bring him right back*, her voice, a small bell, ringing, frightened, over our heads. And I see, now, that was the first of my mother losing her strength.

Anyway, when the chief came round to the house, it was days after the men in slacks and shirts and ties and their sleeves rolled up came down from the county and took pictures and sniffed around delicate as ladies at Sunday picnic before they put him in a gray zippered bag and put the bag into an ambulance that drove off slowly without its lights or siren going, driving off quiet as a dream.

After all that, when things settled down just a little, it was mother who answered the door that morning and after some words I couldn't hear properly, she came to get my dad and Glen from the kitchen. They sent me upstairs to my room. I made the door to my bedroom shut hard in case they were waiting for that and then opened it very quietly and crawled back down the hall on my knees and my elbows like

I SPY to the top of the landing so as to hear what exactly was what.

"No, no, just a few questions," Chief Horton was saying. "Routine." I couldn't see them, but I knew my mother and my dad were sitting on the sofa in the living room because I could see the chief's legs where he was standing, facing that way. I don't know where the other one was or where Glen was, except I figured in the room there with them somewhere.

Chief Horton didn't want any coffee and he'd rather stand. What he did want was just a little understanding of what Glen had been doing that night. *"He was here."* That was my dad's voice sounding strange and high, fear making it go high, I could tell. The chief said oh well, that's what he'd figured, but all the same wanted Glen to tell it. That's when I heard what it was that was in him since he'd come back not the same, heard the sound of it clear and uncovered there in his voice, right under the words. It was *I don't give a damn what you think*, and *There's nothing you can do to me that hasn't been done*, and *Kiss my sweet ass,* all of that sweet and calm, not even a challenge in it, just the fact of it laid plain, saying sure as Jesus, *You've no authority,* though that's not anything he actually said. He just told them about the plant and the black boys that night, about bringing them here and then driving them home. They went on for awhile Glen telling it and the chief stopping for little details all the time. Dad broke in and said, "You can understand. We had to do that. It wasn't right what they were doing to those boys."

"A good Samaritan," said the chief, his voice still mostly respectful. I could tell he was talking to Glen because his legs and his brown trousers and his worn-down-at-the-heel shoes had shifted toward the other side of the room. Glen didn't answer. So they talked some more about what Glen had been doing with his time since he'd been back and all kinds of this and that, everyday stuff and then specific stuff about that night until it seemed things were going round in circles.

That's when the chief told my mother he wouldn't mind that cup of coffee after all. She must have left the room because he started talking again to my dad, saying, "Some weather, huh? Ever summer just seems to get hotter or maybe I'm just gettin' fatter. Heat's hard on a body." And dad agreed, a little relief in his voice, grateful things were still sort of pleasant. Then the chief asked a few questions about my brother's relationship with his passion and Glen said only that he knew her, yes. Then the chief went and said, quiet so I had to strain my ears to hear and with a little we're-all-friends-here in his voice, "I guess over there those people are something else. Cunning little shits is what I hear. You boys have to be hard with them. I understand that. I do." That was to Glen, there was no mistaking that, the chief wouldn't be saying that to my father.

Glen gave him silence. So the chief, his voice suddenly ugly, a little fed up with Glen's attitude maybe, said, "I suppose there's some strange goings on over there. I mean you've seen some serious stuff. That's only natural." Then no one was saying anything and the air down there was sharp as metal and I thought if it had a taste it would be of a nail on your tongue. " I mean it doesn't bother you to talk about this." And nobody's answering him.

After a little of that silence the chief said, "Well, Amos, tell your wife I'll have to have that coffee another time. I got to go now." His legs moved toward the front door and then most of his body came into view, all but his head, and the cop in uniform, I'd forgotten about him, came to stand next to him. The door opened and the uniform left and then the chief says, "You know, son... I don't really give a damn what you were doing that night. But we'll have to see. There may be some who do and then you and I will have to talk some more. You understand. Now, you keep yourself available, you hear?" Then he closed the door after himself quick, not wanting to hear that sound in Glen's voice, that *fuck you*, again, not giving him the chance.

*　　*　　*　　*

It came as a surprise when P. F. Stanley & Co. made their last offer the very next day, the second to last day of August. It was a blow. Dad got his news in a yellow envelope and sat there at the kitchen table muttering in harsh whispers, swearing with lots of s's, like a tree rat I once cornered in the garage. Uncle Aquilla hadn't even let us know it was coming. It was a surprise that P. F. Stanley said in the letter that the men were fired but they could come on back and apply for their jobs if they cared to, but the pay was one dollar less than what they'd had before. They had two weeks to decide. They could come in the fifteenth of September and apply, after that anybody that wasn't hired back was fired forever.

That day I was home and just lurking around the house, staying out of the way, but paying attention. My dad got on the phone and started calling around. *We got to stick together,* he'd say. *We got to stick.* But it sounded like he was talking to himself, and it occurred to me then that perhaps the fight had gone out of him and it was no longer in his nature to be a striker, and I thought of what my mother had said and wondered now if he'd suffer.

That night, in spite of being tired, Mom served

us our dinner. Stuff my dad liked especially—chicken-fried steak, sweet potatoes, mashed with butter, and string beans she'd grown herself. It was a bit of luxury that dinner, laid out with candles, but still my dad didn't eat, just pushed on his potatoes with his fork till they were flat. My mother ate slowly and kept tabs on my progress, making me slow up and put my knife down each time I took a bite, her usual routine, but I knew she wasn't happy.

Glen wasn't there and she'd glance every once in awhile at his empty plate and something in her eyes would kind of fold up and sit down and her brow would wrinkle. Still, she was pretty. I'd heard a man say once, *Now that's a handsome woman—if you like chinks.* Right then my dad was getting more fidgety and tied up in himself and it wasn't long before it got so the air seemed to be sucked out of that room and the summer-dark, hot at the window, seemed about to bust through the glass and come in. So it was a relief when he dropped his fork and pushed his chair back in a rush and stood up and walked out the back door. Didn't say anything to any of us directly, just *I'm gonna take a drive* which he spoke to the ceiling, and I know that hurt my mom because she looked as if she'd been slapped, but she didn't say anything because that was never her way.

I was done, but I sat there with my mom, trying to say, without saying it, that I was sorry for how things were going, and that I was grown enough to understand all the mess, and I could be counted on always and forever. But, she didn't want me there I guess as she said, *You're excused.* And I was about to go on without a fuss because I knew she was about to cry and she wanted that comfort alone.

So it was another surprise for that night when Glen came banging through the back door just as I was about to go. He came in and stood there wavering by the cupboards, holding on to the counter with one hand like he was just lounging, but really to steady himself as he was drunk plain as night and day. His eyes were lit up and burning sharp as a cat's and with the same keen indifference they've got, and I didn't know him that way, even with all his changes and it surprised me and scared me something profound.

But the biggest surprise was that he sneered at mother because she'd started her crying; soft it was and gentle, that crying of my mother. Like it was finally out after a great struggle, only a few tears squeezed out, now, hard as glass, stuck to her cheeks. And those tears made Glen mad, made his lip curl back from the top row of his teeth. "You think losing a job is something to cry about?" was what he said, though it was more of a spit in her direction. And she dropped her eyes because I don't think she could look at his eyes the way they were then. He didn't say anything for a bit, just stood there looking around the room like he'd lost something and as if everything he saw was curious.

Then he said to no one in particular, "You know, this whole sorry town makes me sick. Bunch of ignorant, ignorant fools. Waving ol' Glory. Fried chicken on Sunday, and everything's fine. Just fine. They didn't even give that man a service. The man gets himself killed trying to help them and they don't even say a few words. Too busy pining after some new pickup they can't afford, but will probably buy anyway. Just ignorant shit." He swung round and stares at mother. "I'm surprised they even let you into their church."

Mother stood up and walked past him quickly, out of the room, head down in the old way of her people. Glen sniffed after her, sniffed at the air. "Incense. God, I can't stand the stink of it," he said to himself. Then he put those animal eyes on me for a second, making some vague appraisal, as if I was something too little to eat. He shifted his weight, carefully, so as not to fall, and walked out of the room.

That night I lay in my bed, the moonlight chopped into a rectangle by the shape of the window, making half the room blue. I heard my dad pull up in the driveway and slam the door of the van and come in the house, heard him climb the stairs, each step complaining as he came up, heard him rustling around like he always did in the hallway before he went on down to bed. I lay there a long while. Long enough to hear Glen get up to go puke in the bathroom, and I thought of his passion, that MaryAnn Sheeny, that day in the ditch and I saw those shiny shoes looking like they'd been stuffed with ground chuck, and I wanted to ask Jesus to come into my heart, and I wanted to talk to the ancestors, but that night nothing would come, and, the truth is, words of that kind would come hard ever after.

*   *   *   *

It was a sin. When you do something and you have full knowledge it's wrong there's no excuse for going ahead with it. Choosing it makes it a sin. I knew that when I got up the next day and went into my mother's red room and stole the green vase from the mantel and walked out of the house before anyone was up. I did it knowing my mother was hurting the way she was. And I gave it to that woman.

I didn't even bother skulking around or trying to hide it under my shirt, and I didn't even go by way of the ditch. I just walked along the side of the road, in plain sight, all the way out to her place. I was thinking about how she was pregnant, and I wondered how that baby would look. Wondered if it would look like the Jew or Glen or Uncle Aquilla or some other fellow. I knew it could. I wondered if a woman like that had twins if one could come out one way and one the other. I'd seen that with a shepherd that had one pup that was mostly collie and another pretty close to a lab.

I didn't have the nerve to go up to the door and talk to her, and I didn't really want to talk. I just wanted her to have some bit of beauty, and I knew that vase was special beauty itself and would have to have some effect on her. I went up on her porch, one of those old wooden ones made for sitting, five tall steps up. I set it next to the door like a bottle of milk, a little to the side so she wouldn't break it coming out. I'd thought about a note all the way going over there. *This vase is a beauty, like you* was one. That was too much like romance, not my intention. *The whole world isn't awful* was another, more to my meaning. Of course, I hadn't thought about a note 'till I was already on my way and couldn't make one without any paper or a pencil. I just left it there to speak for itself.

I went back up in the grass and lay down to see if she'd come out and find it. I was up there for a couple of hours, though I didn't mind that. I had lots of practice watching folk's houses and it gave me that excitement a person gets when they fancy they're in charge of things, which they aren't. Pretty soon, the sun came up ragged and burning and the air heated up, dry with the last of August. A million gnats, at least, were doing these little whirligig circuses, moving over the grass.

The trees there were hanging their leaves limp, letting the birds weave in through their branches any which way they wished. I guess as I was lying on my back, I started to think about when Glen showed me, once, how if you're out somewhere completely lost and you're hurt bad and an airplane spots you, you're supposed to lie flat on your back with your arms outstretched so they'll know you need emergency treatment. So I did that. And then she came out.

I heard the screen door squeal first and then spied her stepping out. I rolled over to see. Her hair was piled up on her head, strands falling down her neck, very delicate, and she had a blue housecoat on, something fine and thin, not a farmer's wife's housecoat at all. She came out without even noticing it, came out to the steps and leaned on the post there looking out across the fields kind of soulful. I could just barely see her face proper, her pale flecked skin, half moons of darkness under her eyes. And she did have that baby showing from her stomach, just a little, though it was no more than a puff of air swelling her slip, but I saw how folks had got that notion, that it was true.

She looked sleepy because she lay her head against the post, and I wished right then she would love Glen and make him well. And I could be that baby's uncle, even if it looked like one of those black boys I would be its uncle, and they would have me around, and I would say clever things and they would laugh and be glad of me.

She yawned and turned around, and she saw that green vase. Went over to it and bent down and then knelt down and picked it up and turned it in her hands. Then standing up slowly, she came back toward the steps, looking round, and then stepping down them and walking out a little ways, her face pinched from all that sunlight pecking down at her eyes. I saw that she didn't have that limp any more, and I was glad of it and smiled to myself.

She was sure then that nobody was there but herself so she held the vase out in front of her to study it, the sun filling it up, and suddenly, she pulled it tight, fierce, to her breast, and I knew she knew it was a treasure, and I felt the relief soft in my chest, felt glad of my gift. But that knowledge was also an odd trouble—tasting sin, knowing its pleasure.

*   *   *   *

I had a magnifying glass, and I was round the side of the garage, hunkered down, holding that glass over my hand, pointing a pinhole of sun onto the meat of it. It blistered up good and I thought, *Now, that was dumb*, but some part of me didn't much care, in fact, I could tell that part was happy, happy with itself and with some kind of spite and that surprised me. Then I felt some eyes on me and swung round and looked up and saw Glen's face like the picture of a ghost, framed in the little window there was on the side of our garage.

I stood up. He came round the side of it. He just came up to me, no expression on his face and grabbed my hand and looked at it. Then he tilted his head back, still holding my hand, and stared at the tops of the trees that were back there. He looked back at me and his eyes glazed over sudden and wet. Then he shook his head. And, very odd, no reason for it, he chuckled, no happiness in it, just weird. I yanked my hand back.

He stopped chuckling and threw his arms around me in a head lock and started spinning us round, and we ended up in a crumple on our knees in the dirt. He pushed me all the way down and sat on my chest and started to tickle me hard and half-swat my cheeks, and I punched him in the shoulder, 'cause I knew then that we were playing, but he was scaring me some. Then he stopped and said to me, "You going to knock that off?" And I nodded yeah, sure, OK, and he rolled off of me and onto his back, kind of winded. He goes on lying there, so I lay back, too, and for awhile we just watched the sky that was nothing but the blank of your mind, white and still.

I got bored, and I said, "Glen, what we gonna do?" Though I didn't know exactly what I was asking about.

But he seemed to understand because he put some thought on it, but gave that up and seemed to just flip it, that question, like a coin in his head, then said to me, very serious and true, "I don't know."

*　　*　　*　　*

Summer had hammered us all that it wanted, and come September, the heat just seemed to sift off toward the hills in the distance. The wind blew west from the ocean, over the passes, poured down through the valley, the weatherman said. Dark clouds slid in like slow freighters and the trees and the shrubs would look like big buffalo heads plunging in the wind. When that rain first came, it came at an angle, the wind blowing it sideways, splinters of it hitting the windows. It's not that it rained hard, it's that it just kept at it, out there all the time sweeping across the fields, the streets all shiny and lacquered-up black, the cars whooshing by. Rain is supposed to make you feel sad. Something old about it, all that water being the same water that's been going around since Noah and before. But it made me excited, made me want to breathe in that air, fresh-washed, everything washed, the birds and the houses and the leaves and the sidewalks, and I didn't mind being out in it one bit.

The first week of it, there was lots going on, men coming round to talk with my dad at the table in the kitchen, coming in, scraping their boots, shaking water from their jackets. *God damned dilemma,* is what they'd say, and, *Up shit creek.* Lots came and

97

went, but by the end of the week there were only a few of them Dad counted that said absolutely for sure they wouldn't go in, wouldn't cross a union line now or ever, so help them God, no way, not if it killed them. Most agreed that they shouldn't *cross over*, but that's all they'd said. So everybody would have to wait and just see who was who and what what.

And Glen was becoming a weather unto himself. A boil appeared on his neck one day and didn't leave, his hair came in thick and black and every which way. He never did remember what he'd said that night he was drunk. He wasn't exactly mean, it's just that the trouble that was in him was showing, like a storm you can see building a long way off before it blows in.

He complained that he got intolerable headaches, his body heating up with some kind of burn from inside and he'd have to go be by himself else he would bite you like a dog that's been hurt and does-n't know any better. His trips up to the VA in Fresno weren't a secret anymore. They said he was just over- tired from Nam. But I know he was sure some-thing had happened to his body over there, heard him talking to my folks about it, and I think it made him mad no one completely believed him or under-stood, so he shut up and festered.

Though, sometimes I'd hear him. I'd look out and see him framed in that little window there on the side of our old garage, that was half-falling down, and he was in there whispering to nobody something I couldn't make out. He wouldn't eat with us anymore and came and went at hours strange all the time. Sometimes during the day he'd sit in the doorway of the garage, on an old kitchen chair made of green vinyl and rusted chrome, sit smoking and growing into some place in himself, watching the rain wringing off of the eaves, watching it as if it offended him, personally.

And he called her. Did it at night. At the bottom of the stairs in the velvet chair in the entry. *Think about it*, is what I heard him say. And what she said I don't know, but she took some time saying it because he was quiet, listening, his eyes squinting down and then closing. And he hung up so carefully there was no sound. I know what makes a person go strange, every time; it's something gets them and they can't cut it loose. Gets hooked in them. Like the Plains Indians in my books, those little hooks they put in their shoulders and chests, pulling them up and them twisting, slow in a circle, feet off the ground. And I'd have cut those hooks off Glen, but he'd never have me do it. Like they were all that he had.

I knew also an early rain like that wasn't good, wasn't good for the farms. My dad was saying all the time that the plant might cut production, make them care even less if the men stayed out. Mornings, he'd go out on the front porch to smoke his pipe and put some more of his worry on things. Mother was still gone working a lot or squirreled up in her room. I kept to my room too, reading or drawing or sitting at my window, watching.

I still had my papers to deliver, but I liked walking my route in that weather. And there was choir practice for our concert in the church basement that was coming up soon. Other than that, my time was my own so when the day came I knew I was going to be up and ready to go with my dad to the plant, to see how many would throw all that hardship away and lay the fight down and go in. That Sunday Pastor Jenson spoke out hard about not raising your hand, brother against brother, about how all should remember the Lamb. But everyone knew things could blow up of themselves and all was unsettled.

One night I heard my mother and dad having a fight, sort of a shouting stuffed into hoarseness behind the door of their bedroom. I knew it was about me, about me going or not. I knew it was final when my dad came out of there, slamming the door, saying out loud, *He should understand what this is that we're doing.* And then, *He's going, sister.* He never called her that before.

And it kept raining most unusual. All the ditches were filled and began spilling over in some places, flooding some fields, that water the color of coffee and cream. I started wearing my dad's waders to deliver my route as in some places the water was running down the streets and coming up over the sidewalks and right up to some houses. Folks had sandbags piled around the places that opened into their basements and out round the front doors like little forts a kid might want to play in.

Those nights, truly, I was not sleeping good. I'd think about the strike and what might happen and what it would mean. I'd wonder about Glen and was

100

he ruined, about passion and the black boys huddled in the back of the van. I'd hear that tractor's engine shutting down and huffing diesel over those kittens all tangled, mewling awful in the grass, stripped the way meat is before it's dried, what Glen did once with some of a deer. Sometimes I'd think of the sun, how it was a thorn on the back of your neck all summer long. I'd see that Jew sitting in that tree, half-smiling the way he did, swinging his legs like I remember, except this time—no feet. I'd be wanting him to know I was sorry folks had seemed to have forgot him so quick. I'd imagine him real, swinging like that, but I knew he was dead.

Sometimes, I'd find my mother's face swimming towards me in the dark, her eyes so familiar, her eyes that were the shape of small narrow fish, the irises or the pupils, whichever it is, swelling open, so big I could fly right into them, fly in and float up over the houses, see the chimneys piping smoke, float out high over the fields. I'd see the ditches suffering their limits and the crops and the blossoms, all that grain rotted by rain, and I'd waver there lonely as God, God of the Bible and the ancestors, too. He was there. One night, half awake or asleep, it doesn't matter to me which, I saw Him. He looked a lot like the Jesus framed and hung on the wall of my room, except His eyes were pulled thin, like those of the grandfathers my mother kept on the mantel. And I studied His features, studied them fierce, and all things seemed to be in Him, always, I could tell, all perfectly still, forever, yet all those things changing too, and hurt, there, in that change, always and again, coming like tomorrow and tomorrow and tomorrow which weren't words then, but little brown sparrows bursting new from His tongue when He opened His mouth, when He smiled at me.

*   *   *   *

I think it was a wren that woke me, a little brown fellow, feathers stained dark by the rain. He was scraping his beak on the sill of my window, sharpening it the same way a barber would his razor, sharpen it some, take a look at it and go to sharpening some more. I got dressed quick and went on downstairs. My dad was already up, drinking coffee. I could see by the sink he'd already had the breakfast my mother would've cooked for him before she went to work. I thought maybe he might have changed his mind and was planning on going without me, but he said no that wasn't it, said to hurry it up, said I could have some coffee too, if I didn't dawdle.

I put some peanut butter on a piece of Wonder, without even toasting it, and got it down with some milk, fast as I could. Still standing, I grinned at my dad. *The sap's sure rising in your britches today* is what he said and he was right 'cause my blood was up something foolish, I guess. That day was some day. Outside, it was raw. Still dark when we walked toward the garage, you could feel the wet had got some cold to it. My dad zippered up his yellow slicker and blew air through his lips in a rough whistle. Rain coming so fine it was more of a mist.

Inside the garage, we climbed into our seats, letting the van warm up, dad starting to whistle, nervous, through his teeth a tune I didn't know. The way he whistled was kind of jagged and half-done, him stopping dead sometimes on account he was thinking of something else before he'd recover and start up again. That's him being scared, I thought. My dad never had the same privacy about himself like mother or Glen.

We pulled out of our place, and he pointed the van toward downtown. Engines in those Volkswagen vans weren't big enough to handle the weight is what everybody said and it was true you could feel it straining right up into the seat of your pants. It was loud, too, and kind of a funny car for a family to have.

But, he liked it, liked the big steering wheel that was laid flat as that of a bus, liked sitting up high. I watched him, watched him being scared and still enjoying driving that thing at the same time. My dad was a likable sort, I guess. I think others thought that too, and I was glad of it.

We're early is what he whispered to himself as we pulled up across the street from the plant. Only a cluster of guys were out by the gates, their heads snugged under the hoods of their coats, the wind driving that mist back and forth across them in brief, pushy gusts. It was light out, then, a haze overhead, no specific clouds, just a sky washed the color of tin and some parts flushed pink with the morning that was coming on fast.

We got out and started across the street and it was then I caught fear. Caught the fear of my father. Something about the way he was punching his hands deep into his pockets and rolling his shoulders forward again and again as we walked toward the men. Something a kid might do, pulling his nerve up through himself. I think I realized then, right at that moment, crossing that street which was like any street but was different that day 'cause I think I saw, in those few steps we made crossing, that my dad had been a kid once himself. I don't mean I didn't know that already, I just never felt it before, felt how he could be hurt just as bad as me or any kid by the things in this world. And that's how I caught fear, saw how it was mine all alone, and how I'd have to manage it from then on, same as the next.

We came up close on them and they shook hands all around. I was trying to open the umbrella I'd brought with me. I got it open, forcing the latch, but the wind bent it half over itself, the little web of soft metal in it giving way so that half of the thing was flapping like a tamed crow chained to my head. The guys were stamping the cold from their feet, and talking low, and making these sweeping moves with their heads, looking around front and back of themselves and on occasion spitting off in short, specific arcs and nodding to one another. They saw me struggling with my umbrella and laughed, and I knew it wasn't that it was so funny but because they needed to laugh. Finally, I threw that thing to the ground and let the rain soak me down, wetting my hair, running down my neck to my back.

Pretty soon Erin Bleacher walked out to the gate, wearing a gray poncho, huge as he was, murder in a tent, walking towards us. He didn't say anything, just unlocked the gate, slung the chain off it, that chain ringing loud, and him wrapping it slowly round his fist. And then the cars started coming. They came slow up the street, backed up, bumpers close, headlights on, slow as a funeral. And those cars had most everyone we knew in them. Folks I'd known in our house, folks from church, and Jack's Place. They kept their faces to themselves, eyes straight ahead, not looking at my dad, those few standing with him next to the road.

I wanted to shout what are you boys doing, what's wrong with you, what was the reason you're doing what you're doing, but I did not. And neither did my dad or those few he had. It wasn't long I could watch those men in their cars, so I looked at my dad. He was balled up, worry and more, flicking fast over him, the way shadows work on a face that's staring into a fire, maybe a fire that's burning your house down, except that day it was cold and everything backwards so those shadows were cold. He'd become strange, surely, eyes about to cross, and he saw me looking up at him and a terrible expression closed his face in a way it'd never done before, trying to keep secret what it was that he felt. I glanced down at my tennis shoes and scuffed them along the sidewalk and glanced back. And I saw he was shamed that I knew him, that I was trying to play that I didn't. That'd never happened. I knew we were both different then, though I didn't understand that it wasn't my fault, that we'd just begun what we must, that long growing away from each other.

*   *   *   *

It should be troublesome seeing one still ripe in his age down like that, dead, dead as he was, there in the alley, out back of Jack's Place. I suppose I didn't let myself come up very close to it in my mind, didn't let it into myself, in any way heart-sure, as right then I'd had enough of that. It was on that very afternoon Erin Bleacher came by for a drink after his lunch and just before he would go back to the gate at the plant when the shift would break and the men go home. They said somebody surely hit him, used a hammer or pry bar, but they didn't know who. There were only a few that were there in the rain, looking down on him when I came up with my papers and pressed through to see. The back of his head was cracked open, some of his brain outside of the skull, a clump of it, packed tight as some elbow macaroni you might pull, cold from the fridge. Those curled bits edged in red.

Yet it had some effect on me because I went home directly. I dropped my canvas bag full of papers on the back porch, a few spilling out. I remember looking down on them, watching the ink blot in that rain and run off before I went in. In the kitchen, I took a dishtowel and roughed it over my head, though it wasn't any use, and I knew that as I was dripping steady, little puddles forming up at my feet.

The rain was coming hard by then. Standing there in the kitchen, I listened to the wind throw it sure as tacks, against the house and the windows. I stood there a while, not thinking of anything at all, just hearing the rain, letting it fill me up with its sound. It was a while before I knew why I'd come home. It was the footsteps coming up from the basement that told me. I knew who it was.

*   *   *   *

For a half-second there was surprise splashed like milk over his face when he walked into the kitchen and saw me standing near the sink, back to the window, waiting. He stopped and stood looking at me. He was going out 'cause he had his jacket on and an olive green fishing cap, one of those with the extra-long bill. But he waited on me. Knew I would speak.

"You do that to Erin Bleacher?" I said flat out.

"Who cares if I did?" He looked exhausted and riled, whipped up and careful at the same time.

"You do it?' I asked, again.

"Who'd say he didn't deserve it?"

"How come you know what he deserves?"

He was still looking at me, in spite of the fact that his eyes were fading in and out, seeing me plain and then shifting, unfocused, a little fuzzy, the way a radio station you might dial in at night gets, one that's skipped in across the sky—there and then not. And then I got mad. I hated him, then. He'd ruined himself and done it on purpose and now he was lost. They wouldn't let him get away with what he'd done. Still he stood there. He didn't have a thing to say to me, but he stood there anyway, letting me hate him for awhile, making himself stand there like

108

some kind of penance, giving me that little bit. Even that seemed selfish to me. I grabbed hold of one of the those kitchen chairs there and slammed it over onto the linoleum. My eyes caught sight of my note-book on the counter, and I grabbed it, too, and started tearing it up, ripping out all the pages and throwing them down, half-shredded and crumpled. Then the wind was out of me. "Just...get out of here, Glen," is what I finally said, looking at the mess on the floor and then at him

You'd think I'd had hit him. He was pitiful and wasted in my sight. He waited for more, but I didn't have it so he crossed the room and opened the back door and went out, the door open for a second so the smell of the rain blew in, old as dirt, rotting things now, the room stinking up with the smell it.

*   *   *   *

I didn't need to look. I knew what he'd come for, what he'd wanted in the basement. I knew he didn't have any car, and I knew it would take some time for him to get out to her place. I went into the living room, still dripping, and switched on the television, dialing the sound down. Other than the blue light twitching over the walls there was no light on in there. I sat down on the davenport and gave things some thought. Thought, OK this is some kind of terrible chess and what is my move, what's there on the board? Nobody knew right then it was him that killed Erin Bleacher. In fact, even I didn't know that for certain, though I knew from his face. If I called the police, what then? It was late, the dark already starting to crawl at the windows. My folks would be home pretty soon. But they had no power over him.

That's when I thought of Uncle Aquilla. He'd no love for either Glen or that woman, but he might want to stop him for reasons of his own. He was old, but still strong. I knew that. He had that phony pride big men have in their size, though all pride is phony is what Pastor Jenson said, and he was right in his way, most of the time. That pride might make him go up against Glen. I looked at the TV and saw Walter Cronkite with his tired eyes, full of compassion for what he had to say, his lips moving silently, his mouth saying *Where's your brother?* over and over, though I knew those were words in my own head. Then some shots of a trailer park in Florida came on. A hurricane, I guess. Some close-ups of a housewife doubled-over and crying, what was her house spread out behind her like shredded paper, showing there's lots that's bigger than men in this world. I had to get out of the house.

I ran down the block, the wind and the wet scissoring cold round my ears, the sky failing fast, the storm giving it the look of bath water gone dirty.

The streetlamp, necked out from a telephone pole on the corner, had already come on, that glass, a big amber coughdrop, glowing weak. I ran all the way so when I came on his house I was winded for sure, and I slipped and went down on my knees on the lawn, ribbons of breath going in and out of me sharp. But I could hear him anyway, banging on the front door for Uncle Aquilla to come on and get his fat ass out. It was Glen, and that was confusion as to what he was doing there.

That door exploded inward, and my aunt stuck her head out and told Glen to get off the porch, *right now, lor-dy sakes.* I think that surprised Glen because he backed up some, sort of stumbling off to the side, stepping back past those white columns that stood on each side of the porch. Then Uncle Aquilla stepped out in front of my aunt and shoved her back inside with one of his arms. But she wouldn't go and was fighting him, so he turned round to push her back indoors, and that's when Glen shot him. Shot him once with that old .38. He was, Glen was, crouching there, just next to the porch, off to the side, so when he shot, that little slug caught Uncle Aquilla smack in the side of his butt and spun him round, and he went down, saying, *Oh shit.* But it wasn't so much that he said it as it was punched out of him, like the air smacked out of a paper bag you'd have blown up. Glen looked amazed and turned around and ran up the side of the house along the drive, out of my sight, and it didn't seem long at all he was gone, just a few seconds of Uncle Aquilla moaning and trying to roll himself over and trying to tell to my aunt, who was screaming awful, that he was alright. Then my uncle's Chevy two-ton work truck came squealing down the drive, Glen driving it backwards right out into the street where it slid on the slick pavement in a fast half-circle. He threw it into first, the gears crunching hard, and peeled out of there, quick. I didn't move until then. I didn't say anything to them there on the porch. They never even took notice of me. I just got up and ran.

* * * *

I felt some big something coming up from behind me and turned and saw headlights stabbing that darkness, the rain snowing pale like locusts in the beams. I stopped walking and waited. My legs hurt from the running. I was out a mile or more past our block, in country, on the two-lane of blacktop that went up past her place. The car slowed and pulled onto the shoulder. I stepped over to it as the window came down and saw young Mr. Perch looking out at me, blinking back bits of rain that strayed in to hit him. He didn't say anything, just reached round to unlock the rear door. I nodded, stepped back, and climbed in.

The car was warm and stuffy after being out in the rain. Mr. Cobley and young Mr. Perch had turned round in their seats to get a look at me. "I'm going out to my passion, my brother's passion," I said in answer to their stares. They turned to glance at one another and then after a second when something passed between them, they both laughed some kind of smart chuckle. Young Perch twisted back toward me again, his eyes flicking over me, smiling like a kid who's been naughty. It was quiet and dark in that car except for the push-button radio glowing on the dash and Peggy Lee singing *Is That All There Is?* because that was their sort of station, I guessed. It was strange them out driving in the storm same as if it was a holiday. "Glen's got a .38 revolver," I said. That stopped the smiling.

Yes, I told them Glen was my brother, that's right, the one back from the Marines, but that's all I would give them except that this was strictly family, and I would appreciate the ride and could they get going, please. They had a spat then. Mr. Cobley had wanted to take me home or downtown to the police. *Oh, Val, think how that will look,* Young Percy had said. *I don't give a good goddamn how it looks* is what Mr. Cobley, whose first name was Val, had shot back. I noticed he'd slurred his words some. To that Young Percy had stuck out his bottom lip and and crossed his arms and sunk down in his seat. *Oh, and since when?*

The windows had steamed up and Mr. Cobley rolled a window down and smeared messily at the

113

inside of the windshield with a leather driving glove. *That all you want, pumpkin? Is a ride?* Yes, sir that would do and let's go, could we? And so we did. I had to show them where to stop as there were no lights showing from her house, but I knew where it was from that mailbox that was on top of a post planted in a tire filled with cement at the bottom of her drive. Then those two pulled away, red taillights shrinking like comets, swallowed back whole into the storm, like the secret they were.

*   *   *   *

Lightning branched in the distance, the sky flicking on, sudden, catching the raindrops licking down like millions of stars rushing the earth, then all darkness again. I worked my way up that mud drive and then set out across the grass that grew round her place. I tripped and cracked my knee hard on a rock, and maybe I wet myself then 'cause a warmth slipped down along one of my thighs, and the sky split light again quick, and I saw in a second that held in my head for a long moment what must've been a pheasant or grouse flushing up like a shadow

114

from the grass, swimming, heavy through the air to disappear.

The little house was black. I felt my way up onto the porch and put my ear to the door and listened, but there wasn't any sound I could hear, especially with the drumming of the rain and the wind *shush, shushing* through the trees. I knocked hard as I could, 'till my knuckles hurt, and I tried seeing in through the windows but there was all dimness inside and out.

I decided to go round the back so I slid my fingers along the wood side of the house to keep my balance in the dark, my boots sinking in the earth as I went.

That ground there was mostly clay and it stuck to my boots and with every step my boots grew bigger and more heavy with it. When I came round the back I could just make out the Chevy two-ton and so knew he was there. It was only three big steps up the back porch. I pulled back the screen door that wasn't locked and tried looking in through the back door that was half window, but there was no luck in that. Then the sky boomed and lit up again, and I saw he was in there, sitting on the couch.

I dug into the coin pocket of my jeans and found a quarter. I clicked it against that glass until I thought it might break. Nothing. I was getting tired and I was wet and I was scared. I was angry, too, so I slammed my shoulder into the door and it gave way easily, that wood mush, and I fell in onto the floor. I lay there catching up on myself, on my surprise, feeling the water running off me all around. I struggled up and shut the door, but it didn't seem to want to shut anymore as its latch was broken so I let it be, the wind pulling and pushing it back and forth.

A match struck and tore open a small hole in that room that was dark as a pocket. I saw Glen's face. He was lighting a cigarette. I just watched for a moment as the red end of that smoke traced back and forth from his face to his knee in a slow arc. "Where is she?" I said, my voice striking the air sharply in a way that surprised me. The back door slammed shut and I winced. Then I heard him, chuckling. A funny, soft, rattling laugh.

"You think I came here to hurt her." He paused. "That's it, isn't it?" And he made that funny sound again, a sound like cellophane bubbles slipping up and popping in the back of his throat. "She left two days ago." His voice hoarse.

I came closer, following the sound of it until I could hear him breathing that smoke in and out. His hand was resting on his knee, cigarette glowing like a ruby on his finger. "How come you didn't go with her?"

The cigarette swung up quickly to his face where it pulsed as he pulled on it. "Never wanted me, Dave. That's the whole of it." No sound then except the weather busy outside.

"Why'd you shoot Uncle Aquilla?" I said, though I knew well enough that she must have told him what he'd done, what I'd seen myself all that time back. And I wasn't mad with him anymore. That had gone out of me all of itself.

"You know she loved him. She told me that."

"Uncle Aquilla?"

"No." And he tried to laugh but only a weak cough came.

"Who did she love?"

"Not me," he said, slow, as if still trying to get his mind around the idea.

He dropped his smoke to the floor and must have stamped it out as the little bud of red that it was disappeared. I stared at the floor where it had been. When he spoke again his voice came from the other side of the room, near the front window and it startled me that he'd moved. "You get home," he said, flatly.

"You leaving Glen? You are. I can tell. You got to take me, too. You got to, Glen." I was pleading. I was sounding like a kid and I didn't care, just so as he understood.

"Go on home." His voice soft, though with no feeling, coming again from the other side of the room and also from how many miles out I couldn't count. I thought it could be as far as those birds he'd told me about once, the ones that go up in summer and don't ever come down. Then he was there in front of me, and he pulled me in to himself slowly, my head in his shirt, the smell of tobacco, my head pressed in at his belly so close I could feel him breathing, but he wasn't really there, though we stood there in the middle of the room, the whole world spinning out around us, the two of us, still, in the center of things, outside that rain whipping round, outside those trees held tight by the ground, their tops thrashing back and forth in the wind.

And then he grabbed my coat, and dragged the whole weight of me, sudden and quick, to the front door and with one motion opened it and flung me out where I rolled off the porch and down those steps, my hands, thrown out to break my fall, plunging deep in the mud. I struggled up, breathing hard with the shock, the rain coming hard, wind hard, picked up now to a full, chill blow, me standing there all ashudder, as if I was planted, unable to move like one of those trees.

*   *   *   *

If someone's thinking of you right when they die, wouldn't some part of you get pulled away, too? Seems that could be. I know when someone you know dies some part of all that they were stays in you.

I was halfway across that open space in front of her house, sinking up to my ankles in mud, when I heard it. One sharp thwack like a branch cracking down. That sound snapped my shoulder blades back just the way they would if someone punched me hard in the back. When I heard that gun, and I knew

118

it was a gun, some part of me flew right out of myself and went over the fields, I don't know why, all the way home to that great big eucalyptus out back of our place where we'd skinned that deer all that time back. And that part of me came down slow and settled in quietly, folding its wet wings in the dark. Part of me had all the time in the world then and no place to go. That one cocked his head sideways and looked up, eyes, sharp and wild, laddering up through the limbs, watching, with no thought, the sky there that was streaming fast overhead.

But the other one that I was swung back fast to look at that house. For a long while that one looked before he turned to make his way home and a long ways that was and a very long time it took so that when he got there he was half-dead and just went in through the back door and took off all his clothes and left them pooled on the floor in the kitchen. He took me, the way you might lead a child to bed, climbing the stairs, not stopping at all outside Glen's door, just took me on in to my room so I could get in and cover myself up and shut my eyes, because there was nothing I wanted anymore, nothing to do, then, but wait on tomorrow.

*   *   *   *

Once when I was little I saw a black cat swat a sparrow, deft as could be with his paw. It made an impression on me, I suppose, as I was young, and it had sprung out of the grass, unexpected, like an apparition and swatted that bird, stunning it still and snatching it up with his mouth. And then they were both gone, and all I could see was the long winter grass rippling out in a secretive line as the cat moved along through that field where we were. And then that hint disappeared, too. And I blinked, staring hard, but that grass had nothing to tell. I thought it was that, that cat, nuzzling my face when I opened my eyes and saw my mother, bent close to wake me. But it wasn't like being awake after that. It was all watery and sound-dull, and everything an echo and all a fast vision, and all jumbled, too.

Now we are gathered said Pastor Jenson, head bowed and trusting because *All is vanity, vanity before the Lord. On a hill far away stood an old rugged cross, the emblem of suffering and shame* sang the choir at First Baptist, this time without me, those voices swelling high. *I'm so very sorry*, said Mr. Cobley.

Shot him right in the ass, whispered somebody else. *I don't understand,* said my dad. *Amos, I can't bear this place,* was what my mother said every day after. *Can't-let-you-sleep-any-more* said the rain at my window, whole nights through, tapping it over and over.

*   *   *   *

One day sometime after, I went to the window to see the clouds huddled close as cobblestones on the road that sky was, and they cracked apart ever slowly, and the sun broke through and its swords fanned out, touching the ground with authority. It was October and the rain had quit. Down below, I watched my father, slow and strong because he had to be, crawling in and over the van, roping things down, working like some kind of beetle, with that same sure strength and dumb purpose they have, filling the van with boxes that had in them what things we would take.

I knew my mother was down in her room, the light still trying to get into her eyes, trying to trickle in now, like an electricity that would stutter and fail. I knew my father would load everything first before he came for her and that she would insist on packing the ancestors herself and she would take her time and Glen would go in last and all would be boxed up then and they'd call me, and we'd go.

*   *   *   *

If you drove down Highway 99, all the way down to Bakersfield, you would have found us. Down there, my dad would start work fixing washers and dryers for a laundromat chain. Mother would stay home, fuss some in a sort of half-garden she made there, and sit every evening watching us eat, but not eating herself. She would eat when she was alone, though I never knew why that was. And she would go walking, too much, and she would walk too far, too many times, because after awhile she wouldn't make it all the way back to us and her eyes would become distracted and her mind soft.

It would seem natural for me and my dad to just go along with that, treating her as if she was a child. Never once would my dad admonish her. And though we'd miss her, both of us, there was not anything either of us could do about it, so that was why we never tried, or even talked about it. I guess it

122

made sense to us and so why would we pick at it and who was it that could tell us we should?

We would live then in the middle of town so I would make friends. Arnie would be one, a basketball nut, who, of course, was short and not coordinated at all. He hung with Lance who was tall and mad for girls and thought he knew everything about them because he was into his dad's magazines, *Penthouse Forum* and the like. He would go around in a state of some kind of murderous arousal. He would not once, in the time that I knew him, talk directly to a girl, yet would tell you exactly what they were thinking and in a way that would keep you awake half the night, if you listened to him.

Lance stuttered when he talked, especially if he was excited, which was most of the time. Actually, his whole self was a stutter as he hadn't really grown into his body. When he walked, his long lanky frame would seem to hold back a second and then jerk forward, a little ahead of him, so that he was in a way always trying to keep up with himself. If I had to have friends, and I did because my dad said so, then those two were fine with me. They let me fall in with them without any fuss and didn't ask anything much. I had some fun with those two, but never got close, and that's most everything I remember of them.

Mostly, then, I just walked to school and back. That was Alexander Hamilton Junior High, eighth grade. And the only thing that interested me about school was Melissa Whalen who sat up front of the class. She was a dark-headed girl who hardly spoke up ever unless Miss Watkins called her out directly. Melissa Whalen always answered in a quiet voice, not scared and not showy. Mostly she knew the answers. She would sit in her desk with one leg folded under her and the other hanging down to swing back and forth kind of lazy. After awhile it began to put some hurt on me to watch her, and I would exercise the habit of not looking.

I stayed home most of the time. Dad eventually got on his feet and bought some woodworking stuff on credit—table saw, lathe, drill press and such. He set it all up in the garage. That started me making things out of wood. I liked that. Liked the way the saw would buzz through the wood, make a clean cut without biting. Liked the way things went together, the joints sure with no gaps, liked the smell of the shavings, and the way my hands would heat up when I did the sanding. I never cared what I made. A bookcase was as good as a bowl or a small table. I think I could have stayed in that shop all the time that was mine if my dad didn't come out and say *lights out* every evening.

Once in awhile my dad would cry. Usually that would be at supper, all of us together, mother sitting quiet as any trained animal. Dad would take some particular notice of her and his eyes would tremble and spill over. Sometimes he would put his silverware down and let himself go some, but mostly he would just go on eating, slicing and bringing his fork up to his mouth, the tears coming and him going on with the weeping and the supper as if it was some strange work he had to go on and finish up, like it or not. I never held it against him.

* * * *

One night he came out to the garage, and I felt
him there standing behind me and shut the saw
down to turn round and look at him. He fumbled
along the workbench with his fingers, gathering up
bits of blonde sawdust to his eyes to examine it. He
wouldn't look at me direct. Then said what he came
to say.

"You've had early all that's wrong in this life."

I didn't argue. I wanted him to finish and leave.

"You should think on how you're due for what's
right." I could tell that was hard for him to say, like
he wasn't sure he believed it himself, and I appreciated that he was trying, but that was too much like
caring for me, and I swallowed that back as where it
came from was a place huge with itself.

I nodded and turned back to my saw, but didn't
fire it up, just waited.

"You got as good a chance at that as any, maybe
more," he said, his voice catching.

When I turned back he was gone. It was the last
time he ever tried to really talk with me. That was
nobody's fault, just the way that it was. I didn't
choose my life.

I wondered about Glen. He was born in his body
and he grew into it, had to walk out with it into his

life, his own special self. *Like all those birds,* I'd catch myself saying. The big ones and the small, some of them quick and some clumsy, the wind takes them all, each of them, when they swim up and out to make a way for themselves with their bodies, their beaks and their wings. But the wind shaped them, too. I'd learned that in science. It took a long time, but science has forever. And the wind blows them wherever it wills. Glen was one of those, those birds that wouldn't come down all summer, excepting he could never come down and that is a difference that is no small thing. Those times I wished I still had my notebook, but I knew it didn't matter. I had all those pictures by heart.

I wouldn't cry. But one day I dug a hole in the yard and buried that rifle and my pellet gun, too. I didn't need to talk to the Lord, and I didn't call on the ancestors. I stood over that place, and I made a sign with my fingers, a secret sign of my own that I waved at the sky, my arms over my head. And I felt better after that.

But sometimes, a weight would come on my chest and squeeze me. Those would be the nights I'd come awake to get my breath, and I'd sit up in bed and listen hard, thinking I heard the wind outside in the trees, though those nights were still. It would be then like I was a bowl brimming cold with water from a deep place, a place of lonesomeness, pure.

And I'd feel my heart, a tight bud beginning to open of its own knowledge, slowly, in its own time—like science hinting of the wisdom it must take to make just the petals of a flower. And at times, when I'd wake, my pillow was wet and then, I would just be still and know everything, all, was ordinary and extraordinary—the velvet quiet, the rough blankets, the bush of stars at the window. I would see that Melissa was ordinary, and special, too, only a girl with soft blackberry eyes, set, one and two, in a lean and serious face that was hers all alone. I knew a heart could burst with such sweetness.

And so I would come to know where she lived, would start the watching again, would follow her home a little distance behind, would see the white stucco house with the red tile roof where she lived on a quiet block not more than a mile from school. I would hum the tunes that I'd known, the ones that had gotten stuck somewhere under a rib.

And I felt a little guilty the times I found myself liking some things, like the way the afternoons leaked off, leaving the streets blue in the twilight, my chest tight with that sort of pretty.

Finally, I would come to stand across the street from her house, knowing I had some crying coming someday, that I'd have to open that place in me up, all the way, because she'd already showed me I still wanted it all, the sharp and the tender of things. She would come out her front door and sit on the cement steps. Always in dresses and black patent shoes, and I'd watch.

And one day she waved to me, and I was found out, a blush put on me complete. And I surprised myself. I gave up and did what was in me to do, went on and stepped out from behind that tree. She was smiling then, a little hopeful and unsure. I tell you, just a girl with red ribbons in her hair. And I went ahead and crossed over to her and all that she was, all the hope that there is, a little hesitant, but crossing all the same, knowing the risks, but taking a chance anyway, because I wanted to, because it wasn't ignorance at all.